Anything You Need

Dedication

For my God

Who has given me life
and everything I need to live it

Delight yourself in the LORD
and he will give you the desires of your heart.

Psalm 37:4

Chapter One

"Are you still going to visit Sarah this weekend?"

Brianne smiled broadly and answered Austin's question with a little squeal. "Yes! I'm so excited."

"You just saw her five days ago."

"So? I used to see her every day."

"When are you leaving?"

"Right after school today," she said as the bus pulled up to the school building. "My dad is picking me up, so I won't be on the bus tonight. He's driving me there, and then Sarah's whole family is coming to Clatskanie tomorrow night and will be at church on Sunday morning."

"She'll be at church on Sunday?" he asked, his subdued mood fleeing in a hurry.

She laughed. "Oh? Are you missing her a little too, Austin Lockhart? You just saw her five days ago."

He smiled but didn't admit his excitement about seeing Sarah again. He stood from the seat, and she followed him down the aisle. Once they were off the bus, she decided to tell him something she had been thinking all week, ever since seeing Sarah last weekend when they had gone to Camp Laughing Water for the youth group retreat.

"You know what I think you should do?"

"What?"

"You should write to her. Sarah's a really good letter-writer. Even though I don't see her every day like I used to, I feel like we're closer than ever because our letters are more heart-to-heart than most of our everyday conversations were."

"What do you mean by writing to her?"

"Tell her about your day and anything that's on your mind—funny stuff, serious stuff—whatever. Then when you see each other, it will be like she hasn't been gone."

"Why do you think she would want to hear from me?"

"Because you're one of her friends too, and I think she's having a more difficult time connecting with new people than we're having with her being gone."

Austin didn't comment on her suggestion, but she said one more thing before they parted at her locker. "If you don't want to, then don't. But if you do, I think she'd really like that."

He didn't respond, but she could tell he was thinking about it. Opening her locker and organizing her things, she knew she had a long day ahead of her. Three of her teachers had scheduled tests for today, and she also had to give her oral report in history. She was well-prepared, but speaking in front of a group always made her nervous, and having both Austin and Silas in her class made her feel more nervous about it. Fortunately she had history second period so she would get it out of the way early in the day.

Brooke came to meet her, and they walked to science class together. Of all her tests today, she felt the least confident about science, mainly because they had covered so much information, she didn't know if she could remember it all.

The first portion of the test was fairly easy because it was vocabulary, and all the definitions were listed, she just had to pick the right one. Then there were multiple choice questions which she felt confident about the right answers to except when D said, 'all of the above'. She hated those. At the end they were supposed to write a paragraph about one of the topics listed at the top of the page. Brianne considered writing to be her greatest strength, so she felt good about that part too.

Finishing before some of the other students in her class, she handed her test in and went back to her seat to go over her note cards for her oral report while she waited for everyone to finish. When Silas went to turn in his test a few minutes later, his movement caught her eye, and she watched him walk to Mr. Thompson's desk. He saw her staring at him when he returned to his seat, and he smiled. She smiled in return. His family was moving into the house next door this weekend, and she had become increasingly excited about having him as a neighbor. It seemed strange that by the time she returned from Sarah's tomorrow night they would be all moved in.

After class she walked with Silas and Austin to their history classroom. They both knew she would be giving her report today because this was the last day presentations would be made. Silas had done his on Wednesday, and Austin had done his yesterday. She thought they had both done really well, although Silas seemed to be more comfortable in front of others than Austin.

"You're going to do great," Austin said to her when she voiced her apprehension, and she wasn't sure why, but his simple words really boosted her self-confidence and made her not feel so nervous while two other students went ahead of her.

One of them was Marissa, who didn't seem the least bit nervous, and she spoke very well. Brianne's thoughts returned to the previous evening when Marissa had been at youth group and she shared with everyone how she had decided to make God a part of her life. Pastor Doug had asked anyone to share about something they had learned on the retreat, and even though Brianne felt the decision Marissa had made was sincere, she had been surprised she would share it with everyone like that.

Marissa had also said how she had been the one to help her pray, and that had given Brianne a good feeling. For the past month she had been trying to seek God more and listen to what He had to say, and in that moment she heard God saying, 'Keep seeking Me, Brianne, and I will use you to help others find Me too.'

Sharing about Jesus was something she had a desire to do, but not always the opportunity. He had worked through her last weekend without any specific planning on her part and taken her by complete surprise. She had prayed for Marissa and invited her to come, but that was all until Marissa had come to her on Sunday morning.

When her turn came to give her report, Brianne had just begun to speak the opening sentence when the fire alarm went off. She stood there for a second, wondering what she should do, but as the other students rose from their seats and Mr. Riley did also, she simply followed the others out with her notes in her hands and left the poster she had made on the front easel.

She expected it to be a routine fire-drill and she wouldn't be off the hook from her report, but it did provide some moments where she was able to relax, and by the time they returned to the classroom, she didn't feel nearly as nervous as before, especially because so many of her friends were in the class.

Since last weekend when she'd had a chance to talk to Silas more and had a definite understanding they were just friends, she had felt more comfortable being around him, and she got the feeling he felt the same. When she gave her report, she ended up watching him almost the entire time. He was sitting in the back, so she could look at him easily without feeling like she was staring at him, and yet everyone else seemed to fade away, keeping her from feeling nervous about speaking in front of thirty people who all had their eyes fixed on her.

"How did your report go?" her dad asked after he picked her up from school and they were on the highway heading toward Portland.

"Good," she said. "We had a fire-drill just as I was about to start, so that helped me relax, and then several of my friends are in that class with me, so it was actually kind of fun."

"What friends?" he asked.

"Austin, Marissa, Ashlee, Silas, and a few others."

"Silas' family is moving in tomorrow."

"I know," she said. "It will be nice to have neighbors again."

"Even if it's not Sarah?"

"Yes. I really like Silas—I mean, not like that," she laughed, feeling embarrassed. "He's really nice, and me and Austin have gotten to know him pretty well."

"So everything turned out okay after what happened a couple of weeks ago?"

"You mean Ashlee writing that note asking Silas to the dance and signing my name?"

"Yes."

"Silas talked to me about it, and I told him I do like him and want to be friends but not have a boyfriend or go to dances and stuff with boys right now, and he feels the same way about girls."

Her dad was silent for a moment but then asked her something with a crooked smile on his face. "But if you would have been asking for real, he would have said yes?"

Brianne felt embarrassed, but she answered honestly. "That's what he told me."

Her dad let out a sigh, seeming to not want to have this discussion, but he spoke honestly also.

"I'm not surprised, sweetheart. You are a beautiful and sweet girl, and I knew it was only a matter of time until this day would come."

She smiled and leaned over to give him a kiss on the cheek. "Don't worry, Daddy. I said I'm going to wait until I'm sixteen, and I meant it."

"Yeah, and what am I going to do then? That's less than four years away."

"Pray a lot, I guess. Isn't that what you're always telling me I should do when I'm worried or scared or confused about something?"

"Yes," he said, reaching over to stroke the side of her head and giving her a gentle smile. "Don't grow up too fast though, okay? It seems like yesterday I was rocking you to sleep at night."

"Daddy, I'm twelve and a half. It wasn't yesterday. Beth is your little girl now."

"No, Brianne. You're both my little girls. I'll try not to treat you like you're five, but in my heart you are, and my protective nature is going to be in high gear for the next few years, so I hope you'll be patient with me. Even letting you go this weekend is hard for me, although nothing like last weekend."

She laughed. The look on her dad's face told her he was referring to her being away from home for three days with a group that included boys her age. He had pointed out something when she went to camp this summer, saying even though it was a Christian camp, not all the boys there would act like it.

She had taken his words seriously about not going for a walk or being in a secluded place with a boy she didn't know well, although at the time she didn't think any guys would be asking her to do such a thing. But she felt certain her dad could trust Austin and Silas, and she wasn't sure why, but she wanted him to see them that way.

"Just remember you've been praying for me all this time, Daddy, and I don't think He's letting you down. Austin and Silas are both really good guy-friends for me to have. I trust both of them a lot, and I have a feeling they're going to be watching out for me too. They both were very curious about the time I spent with Joel last weekend."

"I'm sure they were," he laughed.

"I don't mean that," she said, feeling embarrassed again. "It wasn't like they were jealous. They just wondered what we did for an hour."

"And what exactly did you do with Joel for an hour?"

"I told you. He showed me the lookout tower he's building."

"And?"

"And nothing. We sat up there and talked. Joel should definitely be the least of your worries. He's not even interested in girls yet, and besides Sarah, he's the best friend I've ever had. I don't think of him as being a boy—not like that."

"Joel doesn't worry me," he said. "Neither do Austin and Silas. If they remain the way they are now, I would have no problem with you dating any of them."

Brianne couldn't imagine dating Austin or Joel. They were her good friends, and she didn't see either of them like that now, and she wasn't certain she ever could. But Silas—she could imagine that. She wasn't ready for it and didn't want it right now, but she could imagine it.

Chapter Two

"Sarah, your room is huge!"

"I told you so," she laughed. "It's almost as big as my mom and dad's, minus the large bathroom."

"Is Scott's room this big too?"

"Almost. He let me have this one because he knew I would be having friends over more than him."

Brianne set down her bag on Sarah's full-sized bed. She'd had a daybed at the other house, but she had gotten a new one when they moved. Otherwise her room looked about the same as before except for all the extra space in the middle.

"How did your report go today?" Sarah asked.

"It wasn't as bad as I thought it might be. And my English test was super-easy."

Brianne told her about the fire-drill during her report and gave her a rundown of the rest of her day. She also told her about the conversation she'd had with her dad on the way here, and Sarah said something Brianne had heard her say before.

"I think it's so cool you can talk to your dad about boys. My dad just avoids the subject, and my mom says, 'Whatever, honey. I'm sure you'll make good choices.'"

"I think she's right about that," Brianne said, lying down on the bed and enjoying the feeling of the cool and soft comforter underneath her.

"I know, but I wish they would talk to me about it sometimes."

Sarah seemed unhappy, and Brianne wondered if something had happened at school today. She asked her, and Sarah said today had been fine, but not great, like most of her days here so far.

"I didn't think it would be this hard," she said. "I'm used to going to a smaller school where everybody knows everybody and everything is familiar—the way it's always been. It's so different here. Everything. School, volleyball, church. Even this house and our neighborhood. Sure it's nice, but I don't know, it's like I don't fit anywhere."

"I'm sorry," she said, sitting up and giving Sarah a hug.

"Did you feel this way when you moved to Clatskanie?"

"No! I met you on the first day!"

They both laughed.

"How's Silas? Did they get moved into the house yet?"

"They're moving tomorrow."

"Are you excited?"

"Yes. It will be fun having him on the bus with us, and I have a feeling Austin will be going to his house after school a lot."

Sarah's ringing phone interrupted them. She picked it up from her desk, checked the display, and answered with a little smile on her face. Brianne silently wished she could have her own cell phone, but her parents said that wasn't up for discussion until further notice. It was an expense they couldn't justify her need for at this point.

Sarah talked for a minute before Brianne realized she was likely talking to a boy, and she seemed happy about it.

"I can't this weekend," she said. "My friend is visiting me, and we're going out of town tomorrow, but maybe sometime next week."

He said something that made Sarah smile.

"Okay," she said. "Bye, Ryan."

Sarah's shy smile made Brianne curious.

"Who's Ryan?"

"Someone I met this week."

"Did he ask you out?"

"No. Well, not really."

Brianne laughed at Sarah's evasiveness. She wasn't usually like that. "What's going on?"

"Okay, I'll tell you the whole story," she said, coming to sit with her on the bed. She sat with her legs crisscrossed in front of her, the same way she was sitting, and for the first time since Sarah had moved, Brianne felt like they were as they always had been. Last weekend they had been together, but with everyone else too. But for tonight and tomorrow it was just them.

"Last weekend at the retreat I had something I was thinking and praying about I didn't tell you or anyone. Since we've moved here, I've pretty much been ignoring guys who have shown any interest in me because I don't want what happened with Brady to happen here with someone else."

Sarah had told her that before. "Yeah, so?"

"I was starting to feel like maybe that's a mistake. I'm assuming all of them are going to be like Brady, but I know that's not true. I've been praying God would help me find the balance—that I might be able to have some boys as friends like what you have with Austin and Silas."

"Is that what you're trying to do with Ryan?"

"Yes, but the cool part is I just met him this week."

"Why is that the cool part?"

"Because last Sunday I told God I would start being a little more open with any guys who want to get to know me, and I would trust Him to help me know the difference between guys who have good intentions and those who don't, and then on Tuesday I met Ryan."

"Where did you meet him?"

"In the computer lab at school. I was doing research on the Internet, and he came in and sat down next to me. He said 'hi' and I said 'hi' back, and he introduced himself, so I did too, and there was something about him that made me think about what I had decided. So when I finished and he started talking to me, I stayed and talked to him and found out he's new too. His family just moved here this summer from Washington, so we got to talking about how hard meeting new people is, and I found out he goes to church too, but his family is still trying to decide where to go—just like mine.

"And then I didn't see him again until today. We don't have any classes together, but he rides the same bus I do. We didn't know that because I don't usually ride it home in the afternoon, and his dad takes him in the morning, but I was on it after school today because we didn't have volleyball practice, and I ended up sitting beside him. He only lives about three streets over from here.

"On the way home we were talking about our classes, and I found out he has the same English class and teacher I do, just at a different time, and we got this assignment today, so we were talking about that, and he suggested maybe we could work on it together, and since I hardly ever see him at school, I gave him my phone number."

"And you're not regretting that now?"

"No. He's really nice, and after what I prayed last weekend, I think God is a part of it."

"Have you told him you're not interested in dating him?"

"So far I haven't had to. It's like we're both happy to finally know somebody."

"You haven't made any friends here?"

"Not really. I have girls I talk to at school, and I've gotten to know some of my volleyball teammates, but there's nobody I feel close to. And what's really weird is I do feel close to Ryan even though I've only spoken to him twice."

Brianne didn't think she needed to give Sarah any advice or offer her opinion. Sarah always seemed to make good decisions for herself.

Sarah changed the subject. "Okay, enough about boys. What do you want to do tonight and tomorrow?"

"I don't care. Whatever."

"Do you want to go shopping? We can walk to Target from here, and I did some major babysitting this week. People here pay more than I ever got in Clatskanie. One couple who lives down the street gave me twenty bucks, and I was only there for two hours. They have three kids, but they were super-good."

"Do you think they'll be asking you again?"

"They already did. For next Friday."

Brianne had brought a little money along with her, but she didn't have much. She got a small allowance, and she always tried to save it up so she could get something she really wanted rather than spending five dollars here and there and ending up with a bunch of junk she didn't want, but it had only been two weeks since she had made a significant purchase.

She had been hoping to get more babysitting jobs since Sarah had moved away, but one of the families Sarah had babysat regularly for had called and asked her for a night she couldn't do it, and they'd called Emily after her, so Emily had been babysitting for them ever since. And none of the others had contacted her yet.

Brianne's time with Sarah that evening and the following day was really fun, and she was glad she had decided to come even if she had seen her last weekend. Sarah and her family took her home and stayed into the evening when they returned to Clatskanie, and when Sarah's mom and dad went down to their old house to meet Silas' family and see if they had any questions about the house, Brianne went along too.

Silas' sister, Danielle, was in her room and didn't come out, but Silas took her and Sarah down the hall to meet her. They both said 'hello', and Danielle returned the greeting, but she didn't say anything else.

"Nice meeting you," Brianne said before stepping away with Sarah.

"I'm sure she'll talk more some other time," Silas said quietly. "But I wanted her to meet you."

Brianne wondered why, but she didn't ask. They didn't stay too much longer and then Sarah's family dropped her off at the house before going to stay in a motel. Brianne would have invited Sarah to stay overnight except either she or Sarah would have to sleep on the floor. Sarah's daybed at the old house had a trundle bed underneath it, so Brianne had usually slept over there rather than having Sarah at her house.

Sarah was at church in the morning, but her family was having lunch with other people and then would be heading back to Portland, so she had to say good-bye to her there. Last weekend she had felt sad but hadn't cried, but this time she did.

Austin was there to say good-bye to her also, and after Sarah left, he turned to her and said, "You can spend the afternoon with me."

She laughed, knowing he was teasing her and trying to cheer her up.

"Video games, or the skate park? You can pick."

"Thanks," she said. "But I need to go home and get homework done, and see my family since I said I was going to try and do that more."

"Are you coming on Saturday?"

Next Saturday was Austin's birthday, and he had Invited her and a bunch of friends to his party he was having at Pizza Playhouse, a pizza place in Longview where they also had video games and laser tag.

"Yeah, I'll be there," she said.

***

Over the next few weeks Brianne's life fell into a routine. School was school and she continued to enjoy hanging out with her friends and attending youth group on Thursday nights. Austin's birthday was fun, and the following weekend she went bowling with the youth group in the afternoon and out for pizza afterwards, and then Brooke came over to her house to spend the night, saying she didn't mind sleeping on the floor, and she did without complaint.

Brooke was a lot like Sarah. She had been quiet at first and not as open, but that was slowly changing. Brooke was a little more studious and wasn't attracting guys yet, but she was really sweet and fun to be with.

Whenever she spent time with her, Brianne never felt like Brooke tried to tell her what to do or gave her bad advice, and she was the type of person to follow the rules, be nice to everyone around her, and was usually in a good mood.

The following weekend her parents went to a conference and left her semi in-charge of her siblings. It was the first time they had ever done that, and Brianne found it to be more work than she anticipated. One of her mom's friends came over several times a day to check on them, and with Silas' family living next door, she had someone she could call if there was some kind of an emergency.

One of the high school girls came to stay with them at night, and she reminded Brianne of Joel's older sister, Megan, so she didn't mind having her there, and she had a chance to talk to her on Saturday night after Beth and her brothers had gone to bed. She thought Grace was pretty and sweet, and she found herself hanging on her every word. She seemed to know so much about life, and she had great stories to tell about trips she'd gone on with groups from school and things she did with her friends and her experiences with guys so far. Grace didn't currently have a boyfriend, but Brianne knew she had dated a couple of guys in the youth group before, and she asked when she had gone on her first date.

"It was during my sophomore year," she said. "I went to a Friday night football game and then to the dance afterwards with a guy at school. He was nice, and I knew him pretty well, but after I got home I remember having an uncomfortable feeling that he wasn't the kind of guy I should be dating. He didn't go to church, and even though I thought maybe I could get him to come with me, I knew that probably wasn't the best way to lead him to Jesus. So when he asked me out again, I told him I just wanted to be friends, and we still are. And he's even come to church a few times with James who knows him too."

"And you dated James for awhile, didn't you?"

"Yes. For about three months. He's a super-nice guy, and I enjoyed going out with him, but I didn't feel like we fit together. So now we're just friends."

Brianne didn't expect her to, but Grace fired a question about boys back at her. "Who do you have your eye on, Brianne?"

She laughed. "No one. I have some guys as friends, and I think they're cute and nice, but I'm not ready to be their girlfriend."

"That new boy is really cute. What's his name?"

"Silas."

"If he was my age, I'd be doing serious flirting with him."

Brianne smiled. "He's really nice too."

"I think you have plenty of time to figure that out. The best relationships I have with guys right now are those I haven't dated, so don't be in any hurry."

Grace looked past her, and Brianne turned to see that Beth had gotten out of bed—again. Grace took care of it, picking Beth up and taking her back to their room.

"I'm glad you could stay with us this weekend," Brianne said when she returned. "I'm used to watching after my brothers and sister when my mom and dad go out for an evening, but they're usually back in time to put them to bed. I think they listen better to you than me."

"I'm glad I could be here," she said, "and your parents are paying me nicely for my time, so I don't mind."

Brianne went to bed shortly after that, and she couldn't help but feel a bit miffed her parents were paying Grace to be here for a couple of hours in the evenings and sleeping here, when she had been doing everything by herself the rest of the time, and they weren't paying her a thing.

She knew she should see it as a part of being in this family, not like a babysitting job, but she'd had to turn down two other jobs for this weekend from families she had been waiting to call her. There were times she really hated being the oldest of five kids.

Thinking about the letter she had gotten from Sarah yesterday only made it worse. Sarah had been babysitting regularly for the family who paid her really well for her time, and she had gotten another regular job this week. One of their neighbors had two girls, and the mom was pregnant with a third child. Sarah had babysat for them a few times, and this week they asked if she could start coming over a couple of evenings each week to help with laundry and other household chores because the doctor had told the woman she needed to stay off her feet as much as possible until the new baby came. Sarah had agreed to do it because volleyball was ending this week, and they were going to be paying her for being there to watch the girls plus the housework.

It's not fair! I only get my dinky allowance for doing that stuff all the time! She began to wonder if it was time to have a talk with her mom and dad about how much she did around here and demand a raise instead of being treated like a slave in her own house.

Chapter Three

On Sunday morning Brianne got up and went to church like usual. Her parents wouldn't be getting home until this afternoon, but Grace drove them in the van, and they each went to their own classes. One of her parents' rules for the weekend was she couldn't have any friends over to the house while they were gone, and to keep any phone calls to a minimum, so she was happy to see her friends and talk to them without having to wonder what her younger siblings were up to.

But about ten minutes into the youth worship time, someone came to the youth room and tapped her on the shoulder. It was one of Beth's teachers, and she had Beth in her arms. Beth had been crying ever since Grace had dropped her off at her class.

Brianne took her from Mrs. Weber's arms, and when she stepped away, Brianne wasn't sure what to do. Beth was calm, so Brianne held her until the music stopped, and then she sat down with Beth in her lap.

"Do you want to go back to your class now?" she whispered.

Beth shook her head. "I want Mama," she said loud enough for others to hear.

"Shh," she said, holding her close to her chest. "Mama's not here. You can sit with me."

Beth was good and didn't make a peep while Pastor Doug made announcements. When it was time to go to the junior high classroom, Brianne decided to stay in the main room with the high schoolers because she figured it would be easier to stay where she was, and she also knew she would feel awkward being in the other tiny room with her little sister in her arms.

Grace came back to sit with her and tried to coax Beth to come to her, but Beth didn't want to, so Brianne said she would stay. The thoughts Brianne had been having last night returned. How could her parents leave her for a whole weekend, and not only that, but leave her in charge? Why not send them to her grandparents, or take Beth with them and let her and her brothers stay with friends? She had gotten very little homework done and hadn't started writing her book report that was due tomorrow.

When her parents had first told her they thought she was ready to do this, it had made her feel grown up. But now she felt used and abandoned. *It's like I'm Cinderella, only it isn't my wicked stepmother who's making me work hard for nothing, it's my own mother!*

By the time Grace drove them home after the church service, Brianne felt so tired she didn't want to think about having to make lunch for everyone, folding the last of the laundry she had promised her mom she would do, and clean up the house her mom had left perfectly clean on Friday afternoon but now was a disaster.

She thought maybe Grace would stay to help her out, but she didn't. Her responsibility of spending the night with them and taking them to church was complete, and she was free to go hang out with her friends and probably go shopping or something. Grace didn't even have younger brothers and sisters. She was the youngest.

After making a simple lunch of peanut butter and jelly sandwiches and grapes, which all three of her brothers complained about for different reasons, she took the laundry out of the dryer, folded it, and put it away. She almost left the house as it was. She wasn't the one who had made the mess, it was her brothers, and if her mom and dad came home and saw their stuff in places it didn't belong, they would get in trouble, and she would be able to tell them what a terrible weekend she'd had with those three disgusting creatures she was forced to live in the same house with.

"J.T.!" she called out, deciding she would at least make the effort to have them help. "Jeffrey, Steven, can you come here please?"

No response. She could hear them playing video games in the living room. Leaving their room and going down the hall, she called them again and none of them looked at her, but at least J.T. responded.

"What?"

"You guys need to clean up your room before mom and dad get back. And this room too."

"Why us?"

"Because it's your mess!"

"So?"

"So! I'm in charge, and I say so."

She went to the kitchen to do the dishes. She had cleaned off the table and had everything else looking pretty good before her brothers had moved from the floor in front of the T.V.

She gave up at that point. If they wanted to get in trouble, that was their choice. She had homework to do and a book report to write. Going to her room, she stepped through the doorway and immediately knew something wasn't right. She had laid Beth down for a nap after lunch, but she wasn't in her bed.

"J.T., do you know where Beth is?" she asked, going back into the living room.

"Huh?" he said without looking at her.

"Beth. Our little sister! Do you know where she is?"

"Haven't seen her."

She began searching the house, calmly at first and then more frantically when she didn't find her in her brothers' room, or her parents', or the bathroom. The house wasn't that big, where could she have gone? She checked everywhere again, and then ran outside, searching the yard and scanning the large field that was behind their house. No sign of her.

She went back inside. "J.T.! I can't find her. Could you help me, please?" She started crying, and J.T. finally turned to face her.

"Uh, sure," he said, getting up from his spot. "Where have you looked?"

"Everywhere!"

"She's not in her bed?"

"Of course not! That's why I'm looking for her!"

J.T. calmly walked away, stepped into the hall, and Brianne followed him. She had already checked all the bedrooms, but she didn't know what else to do. J.T. went to his room, stepped across the floor littered with toys and clothing and slid open the closet door. Beth was lying there on the floor fast asleep.

"There she is," he said as if he'd just found a missing sock instead of their precious little sister. "She's been sneaking in here all week during her nap time. Mom's not sure why, but she told us to leave her alone."

Brianne wondered how J.T. knew that and she didn't. She got home before her brothers, and Beth was usually awake by then. But then she remembered J.T. had been sick and stayed home two days this week.

"Thanks," she said. "I didn't know she had been doing that."

She stood there looking at Beth for a minute, letting the tears fall because she knew she was safe, and because she was reminded of how special Beth was to her. Her only sister. The one who often crawled into bed with her in the middle of the night. The one who had sat quietly on her lap today during church because she missed Mama but felt secure and loved in her arms.

Closing the closet door partially, she went to her room, and the messy house was forgotten. Her brothers couldn't clean their room right now with Beth in there anyway, and suddenly it all seemed unimportant. She knew her mom often didn't keep the house looking perfect, especially on the weekends when everyone was home.

By the time she finished her book report, Brianne knew her mom and dad would be home in a little while, and she decided to do one of the studies in her devotional book, *Heaven In My Heart*. She had been doing one every other day. The other times she was doing her own reading in the Book of Matthew, but she hadn't done either since Wednesday night. She'd had youth group on Thursday and hadn't taken the time on Friday or yesterday.

The lesson for today was about loving others, and she read some verses in John 15 where Jesus is speaking to His disciples. Verses 11 and 12 said, *"I have told you this so that you will be filled with my joy. Yes, your joy will overflow! I command you to love each other in the same way that I love you."*

Brianne was reminded of something Pastor Doug had talked about on the retreat last month. Along with deciding to make her family more of a priority, she had also learned loving others was a direct result of her relationship with God. And she could see how not spending any focused time with Him for the last three days and never asking for His help this weekend had left her feeling tired and grouchy this afternoon.

She spent several minutes thinking about one of the questions related to her relationship with God and how she saw Him.

Do you believe He loves you? Has He given you
any reason to doubt His love for you?

Brianne remembered her thoughts about feeling like her mom and dad had abandoned her this weekend, and she supposed she felt God was responsible for that. After all, they were away because they were at a ministry conference to help them learn more about serving others in their church and community, and He was the one who had given her these irresponsible, unloving parents in the first place!

She wrote out her honest thoughts, and then she continued reading:

Believing we are loved by God is necessary to loving Him back, and it's also the key to loving others. Why? Because when we believe we are loved by an almighty, loving God who will always care for us even when others don't, then it really doesn't matter how others treat us. We don't love them because they love us. We love them because God loves us. And with God's help, we can love anyone because His love for us is that huge! Believe you are hugely loved, and you will love others hugely too!

Brianne highlighted the final sentence and continued reading. Further down the page she highlighted several more:

Jesus says believing we are loved and loving Him and others in return will make our joy complete. Loving others makes us feel good. So if you're feeling bad, maybe you need to take a serious look at yourself. Are you accepting God's love for you? Are you passing that love on to others?

At the end of each devotional the author often asked the question: *What do you hear Jesus saying to you today?* In her journal Brianne wrote:

I know you love me, Jesus. I haven't acted like it too much this weekend, but I know one of the greatest ways you have shown me your love is through my family. I love them, and I know they love me. This morning I was feeling frustrated with Beth because she was being so clingy and didn't want to go to her class, but when I thought I'd lost her, I realized she is a huge part of my heart. And I know I would have reacted the same way if it had been Steven or Jeffrey or even J.T. who was missing.

But even if I didn't have a loving family, I know your love would still be here and would fill in the gaps others had left. With all the terrible thoughts I've been having this weekend, yelling at my brothers, thinking my parents need to pay me after all they've done for me, and not spending time with you for three days—you still love me. Help me to remember that and to love others the way you love me.

She knew as soon as her parents came in the door because she heard Steven yell: "Mom! Dad! You're home!" in his usual exuberant way. Brianne laid her journal aside and went into the living room where her mom and dad were giving hugs to her brothers.

Stepping across the room, she didn't have to wait for her turn once she reached them. Her dad hugged her first, and then her mom, and they both said the same thing. "Missed you, honey."

"I missed you too," she said, not because they were home now and she didn't have to be in charge anymore. She missed them because they were her parents who loved her so much, and she couldn't live without that love for even a day.

"How did it go?" her mom asked.

"Fine. I thought I lost Beth this afternoon, but she was napping in J.T.'s closet."

"Oh, yes. I forgot to tell you about that."

"She didn't want to stay in her class this morning either, so she sat with me."

Her mother didn't seem surprised. "I thought about having her go with us, but I knew she would be just fine with her big sister here to look after her."

Chapter Four

Okay, Brianne. I feel like I have to be honest with you. On the retreat you told me you wanted to make an effort to spend more time with your family, and now you're writing me this letter wishing you could get more baby-sitting jobs for real money instead of having to baby-sit your brothers and Beth for nothing? What's that about?

Okay, I just had to get that off my chest. Guess what? Austin wrote me a letter, and it was actually a really good one. He said he would like us to start writing to each other. Do you know why he's doing this? Did he say anything to you about it? Just wondering.

I went to my neighbor's house today to watch her girls while she rested, and she had a few chores for me to do, but not too much. I had fun. Her girls are really sweet. Oh, and by the way, you do not want to baby-sit the Goodman boys! They are not good! I was going to warn you about that before but I forgot.

I do think if you want to ask your mom and dad for a bigger allowance that would be okay. I don't think they would see it as being disrespectful as long as you don't argue with them over it if they say no. I can understand your frustration, Bree, but I know you love your family and they love you, even if it doesn't seem like it sometimes.

Brianne smiled at Sarah's honesty, feeling grateful to have a friend who would hold her to a decision she had made last month. And she also smiled because she felt totally different about the whole thing now. She had decided not to say anything to her mom and dad about paying her for watching her siblings over the weekend, and they had surprised her with a bonus to her normal allowance. She had decided not to ask them for a raise either, and she felt like God had blocked that feeling she had been struggling with the last few weeks of wanting more money. All the things she had wanted to buy before suddenly seemed unimportant, and her joy-level had definitely increased since Sunday afternoon.

Going inside the house after petting Whiskers and Molly, she saw her mom on the couch reading to Beth. She put her backpack in her room and returned to take her mom's place, and her mom thanked her.

"How was school today?" she asked, rising from the couch to tidy up the room.

"Okay. We're doing a fundraiser for band, and we're selling Christmas wrap this year. Do you want to buy some?"

"Sure. Did you talk to Silas today?"

"Yes. Why?"

"His mom called me this afternoon and said Danielle didn't come home last night. Did he say anything to you about it?"

"No." She thought for a moment and then said, "He did seem a little down today though. I wonder why he didn't say anything?"

Brianne debated about calling Silas both before dinner and after. She tried at seven-thirty, but there was no answer at their house. In the morning when he walked down the street to meet her at her driveway and wait for the bus, she asked him about it, and he said Danielle had come home late last night.

"Where was she?"

He shrugged. "She didn't say."

"I'm sorry," she said.

He didn't respond, and he remained on her mind for most of the day. Remembering the devotional on loving others she had done a couple of days ago, she wondered how she could best be a friend to Silas in this. Was there anything she could do?

She talked to her dad after dinner, and he had a suggestion that surprised her, but she liked it. "You should take him somewhere and have some fun."

"Just me and him?"

"Sure, or maybe Austin too."

"Where?"

"The movies, bowling, Pizza Playhouse—or are you too old for that now?"

"Pizza Playhouse? I hope not," she laughed.

"You should take him there."

"That sounds like a date, Daddy."

"It doesn't have to be a date if you're just friends. Have Austin go too if you want, but don't turn it into a big group thing where a bunch of you go somewhere. Make it special for him—let him know that's your intention."

"Okay. Will you drive us?"

"Sure. Let me know what time you're thinking so I can check my schedule."

She told Austin about her dad's suggestion the next day on their way to the band room when Silas wasn't with them. He liked the idea too and agreed to go, but he thought they should let Silas decide where.

"Do you want to ask him, or should I?"

"I think you should," he said.

"Why?"

Austin smiled. "I think it would be more special coming from you."

"Okay," she said, feeling unsure how exactly she was going to ask him. She didn't want to give him the wrong impression, like she was asking him out, but she didn't want say, 'So, me and Austin are going to the movies on Friday, want to come?'

She was still trying to rehearse her words in her head when Marissa sat beside her. She took out her flute, and Brianne said 'hi' and asked her if she was going to be at youth group tonight.

"Yeah, I was planning on it," she said.

"Do you want us to pick you up?"

"Yes, if you can. My dad doesn't usually want to go anywhere once he gets home."

Marissa's mom was doing better but still recovering from her latest battle with Bulimia. Brianne had noticed Marissa handling it different emotionally since the retreat. There were some days when Brianne could see they had been having some rough days, but mostly Marissa seemed a lot happier. And Brianne knew for sure she was making better choices about whom she spent time with and where, and one of her best friends had come to youth group the last two weeks.

"Is Kayla coming tonight?"

"I think so. She usually goes home with me after basketball practice, so unless she can't for some reason, she should be there. She really likes it. Her parents are Catholic, and they go to Mass on Saturday nights, but she likes youth group too."

Miss Duncan got class started by asking how they were doing on their fundraiser. Brianne hadn't gotten started yet. Her mom had looked through the catalog last night and picked a few things—Christmas wrap and a few small gifts. There was a butterfly calendar Brianne thought she might get Sarah for Christmas, and there was also a coloring book and crayon-set she wanted to get for Beth, but otherwise she didn't expect her sales to be too high. She hated trying to sell stuff to people.

By the time she boarded the bus that afternoon, she had in mind what she wanted to say to Silas once they were off the bus. He seemed in better spirits today, and she wondered if this was really necessary, but before she checked the mailbox, she kept him from saying a quick 'see you later'.

"After what happened with Danielle this week, I thought you might need a fun night out. Me and Austin were thinking we would like to do something, just the three of us. Do you want to go?"

"Where?"

"You pick. The movies, Pizza Playhouse, whatever you want."

He smiled. "You're asking me out?"

She smiled in return, knowing he was teasing her. "Yes. I'm asking you out—me and Austin."

"You're not really Ashlee dressed as Brianne, are you?"

"No," she laughed. "I'm serious. Just a fun night out with your two best friends. What do you say?"

"I say yes. But why are you doing this?"

"Because we care about you, and we know all of this is harder on you than you're letting on. Isn't that what friends are for—to be there when we need each other? I wish I could do more, but I know I can't, so this is my best offer."

"When?"

"What's good for you? My dad said he would drive us."

"Anytime is fine," he said. "I don't have any plans this weekend."

"Okay, I'll find out when the best time for my dad is and let you know, okay?"

"Okay. Thanks, Brianne. I don't know what to say."

"You don't have to say anything. I'm sure you'll be there for me and Austin if one of us ever needs anything."

By youth group that night it was all arranged. The best time for her dad was Saturday evening, so Silas decided he wanted to go to Pizza Playhouse for pizza and video games. She wrote a letter to Sarah before she went to sleep, telling her about it. She had also gotten a letter from Megan today, and she wanted to write back but decided to wait until the following day, and she also wrote a letter to Joel. She had written him once since seeing him last month, and he hadn't written her back, but she wrote him again anyway.

Dear Joel,

Hi. Should I assume you fell off a cliff since I haven't heard back from you? Megan didn't mention anything about it in her letter, but maybe she forgot. Just kidding. I know you're not a big writer, but I want to tell you about my life—even if you don't really care.

She went on to tell him about her weekend of being in charge while her parents were away and what she had learned through that experience. She also reminded him they were going to be coming down to visit on Thanksgiving Weekend which was only another month away.

Do you have that lookout tower finished now? That's the coolest thing ever. I mean that, Joel. I think about it all the time. The view was amazing, and there was something special about being up there with you, but maybe that's just me. You're probably like, 'Oh, did I take Brianne up there? I don't remember.'

Actually you're probably wondering who is writing you this insane letter! 'Brianne who? I never write to anyone named Brianne, why is she writing to me?'

Love you
(even if you don't write),
Brianne Rebekah Carmichael

Chapter Five

On Saturday afternoon Brianne got a phone call from Austin. He was sick and couldn't go to Pizza Playhouse with her and Silas.

"Are you really sick, or are you trying to set us up?"

"I'm really sick. I have a fever. Do you want to talk to my mom?"

"No, I believe you. Do you think we should still go or wait until next weekend?"

"I think you should go. Have fun, Brianne. Don't go all weird on him just because I'm not there. Be yourself; that's who we both like."

She smiled. "Okay. But if he tries to kiss me, I'm holding you responsible."

"He won't, Brianne. He's told me several times how glad he is you can be his friend without it having to be a boyfriend-girlfriend thing."

Brianne was glad Silas felt that way, and it helped her to not get too nervous about tonight, but as she got ready while the rest of her family ate dinner, she did spend a little more time paying attention to her appearance and clothing choices than she normally did.

Standing in front of the bathroom mirror, she decided to wear her hair the way she did most of the time, parting it slightly to the side and letting the blondish-brown strands hang straight. Her hair was all one length, and she didn't have bangs. She decided not to put on any makeup because she didn't normally wear any to school or when she was just hanging out with her friends.

Her parents had made her wait until she was twelve to start wearing any, and she had looked forward to it for about two years, but then when she finally could, she didn't really like it. It took too much time in the morning and made her face feel itchy, especially when it was warm or she got sweaty from running during track practice or in P.E. And it also seemed to make her break out more, so she only wore lip gloss sometimes and used a cover up cream when she had a pimple.

She brushed out her hair and put on a bit of hairspray to keep it from falling into her eyes, and then she brushed her teeth. Going to her room, she decided to wear her pink jeans and a white pullover shirt with a pink hood on it and long pink sleeves. It was an outfit she often wore on Fridays to remind Austin Fridays were pink days.

Her dad drove her to Silas' house when he finished eating, and she got out of the van to meet Silas at the front door. After saying a brief hello to his mom and dad, she told them when they would be back, and Silas followed her to the van. They were able to be themselves on the drive to Longview, and once they had ordered their pizza and found a table to sit at, she felt completely at ease. She asked him if they had someplace like this where he had lived before, and they had Chuck E. Cheese's in the nearest large town, which was similar, and he'd had a birthday party there once, just like she and some of her friends had done here.

They waited until after they ate to play games, and Brianne had a lot of fun. Silas wasn't into video games as much as Austin and her brothers, so he wasn't as good, and they were more evenly matched. They also played Skee-Ball, which was her favorite, and she generally did better than he did, but she mostly had fun because Silas was fun to be with.

Her dad was coming to pick them up in twenty minutes when Silas asked if they could go sit and talk for the remainder of their time. They were both out of tokens and had cashed in their tickets for some prizes. She had gotten a small stuffed kitty for Beth and something for each of her brothers, along with a colorful pen set for herself.

They found an empty table and sat across from each other. Brianne waited for Silas to speak. He had been acting like his normal self all evening, and she hadn't felt like he was hoping for more with her than their simple friendship, but she wondered if that was about to change. She hoped not and said a silent prayer she would be honest and say what she really wanted to say, not what she felt like Silas wanted her to say.

But it wasn't about them and their relationship. It was about his sister. He had something he wanted to tell her.

"Up until she was fourteen, about halfway through her eighth-grade year, Danielle was a lot like you."

"Me?"

"Yes. She was really involved in youth group, and she was a good big-sister to me and nice to her friends. She wore her hair the way you do and dressed like you, and if someone would have told me she would be like she is now, I never would have believed them."

"What happened?"

"One of her church friends made her mad about something. It had to do with a guy they both liked, but I never heard the whole story. She stopped going to youth group to avoid being around her, and then she started doing a lot more things with her friends from school. She started dressing like them and going places she shouldn't, and then she started dating Vince, and by that summer she was a completely different person. All of her church-friends had taken the other friend's side, and so she didn't have any Christian friends anymore, just the new ones."

"Wow. I guess people can change fast, huh?"

"Yes, and I would hate to see something like that happen to you. When that whole thing with Ashlee happened, I was really afraid I was going to end up being the cause of a big fight between you. I'm glad it didn't turn out that way, but that doesn't mean it might not turn out differently the next time."

Brianne understood what he was saying, and she knew her relationship with Ashlee still wasn't the greatest, but she thought that was more Ashlee's fault than hers.

"Don't you think Ashlee is more likely to end up like your sister than me?"

"Maybe, but my sister was like you, Brianne, not Ashlee. Her friend who betrayed her was like Ashlee."

"Oh."

Silas reached across the table and took her hand. "You're a really special girl, Brianne. You're like Danielle used to be, and she's not listening to me right now, but I hope you will."

She smiled. "I'm listening."

Silas released her hand, and she told him about her weekend of taking care of her siblings and what she had learned from her bad attitude.

"I feel like God is teaching me about being a big sister, not just having brothers and sisters, and about being a friend, not just having friends, you know what I mean?"

"Yes."

"That's why I brought you here tonight. I wanted to show you I care and that I'm here, as a friend, for whatever you need."

"And that's why I'm telling you this," he said. "I care about you, and I'm here for you, as a friend, for whatever you need."

Before Brianne went to sleep that night, she wrote Sarah a letter, telling her about her time with Silas and what he said about his sister. She had already done her devotional book earlier in the day, and she shared something she had learned relating to what Silas had said about letting things like an argument over boys coming between friendships, and then she added her own thoughts.

I think it comes down to trusting God. I'm not always going to be able to trust Ashlee, and even some of my closer friends might do things that hurt me sometimes, but no matter what someone else might do to me, I can always trust God to take care of me and make everything okay. Like when Ashlee wrote that note to Silas and you told me to love her anyway. I didn't see how I could at the time, but now I'm glad I let it go. God has used it for good. He's made me and Silas closer friends because of it.

And I'd like to echo Silas' words to me. I care about you too, Sarah, and I'd hate to see you end up like Danielle. I have a hard time imagining that—even more so than me—but I know it could happen. So if you're ever struggling, I want to know about it so I can help. We might not live in the same town anymore, but we can still be here for each other. You've already proven that to me. And for anything you need, I'm here too.

In the morning, Brianne purposely sat beside Ashlee at church when they went to their classroom for their lesson-time. She had been avoiding her. Not to the point where she didn't want to be at church if Ashlee was there, but she knew one more selfish act from Ashlee could send her down that road.

She did the same thing on Monday at school and throughout the week, acting as if Ashlee had never hurt her and truly letting it go. Not because she trusted Ashlee. She knew she had every reason to not trust her. But she trusted God to take care of her no matter what Ashlee or anyone else did to her in the future.

On Saturday she wrote another letter to Joel. She had thought about it last weekend after talking to Silas, but she had decided to wait to see if Joel wrote her back this week. But this was too important to keep to herself, so she told him about what Silas had said and that she wanted him to know she felt the same way about him.

> *I don't just see you as someone I grew up with. I see you as one of my best friends, and I know we're both heading into what could be some really tough years for us if we make the wrong choices. So don't! You're too special to throw your life away over drugs, or a bad relationship with a girl, or withdrawing from your family and friends.*
>
> *I'm here for you, Joel, for anything you need. Always. Even if I haven't heard from you in five years and you suddenly need me, okay? And I also know God will always be there. Even if you mess up, you can go to Him and find*

forgiveness and let Him make things right. Promise me you'll remember that?

I'm not trying to say I think you're going to make bad choices. In fact, I'll be really surprised if you do, but I think if we admit to ourselves it could happen, we'll be less likely to let it.

I love you!
Brianne

"Love each other as I have loved you."
John 15:12

Chapter Six

Brianne wrote Joel's address on the envelope and hurried to the mailbox through the rain falling on the November day, but the mail for today was already there, so Joel's letter wouldn't go out until next week. A letter from Sarah was waiting for her, and she ran back to the house, taking the letter inside to read.

Sarah sounded better. Her family had decided to try another church because the one they had been going to was too big for them to feel comfortable there. Sarah thought the youth group was too cliquish, and both she and Scott had found it difficult to make friends. She and Ryan were still getting to know each other, and his family was currently going to a church they liked, so her family was going there tomorrow.

Checking the time, Brianne knew she needed to get ready. The youth group was meeting at the church this afternoon to paint classrooms, and afterwards they were going to Pastor Doug's house to have pizza and watch movies. On Thursday night Marissa had said she wanted to go, so they were picking her up.

She spent most of the time with Marissa. Marissa's friend who had been coming to youth group hadn't been able to come today, and neither Brooke nor Emily were there either. Ashlee rarely came to anything involving work, but Marissa was the opposite. She loved helping and was often the one volunteering at school to do things that required leadership and organization. She had always been on student council, and she had been voted vice-president of their class this year.

She was fun to work with and not bossy. While they were painting a classroom together and making significant progress, Brianne asked how things were at home.

"My mom is back at work, but it's hard to know if she's really getting better or faking it, and my parents are having problems with Miguel."

Marissa had two older brothers. Miguel was fifteen, and Josúe was eighteen. "What's been going on with Miguel?" she asked.

"Normal stuff. He comes home later than he's supposed to sometimes, and his grades haven't been great lately. I don't think he's in any serious trouble, but he has a girlfriend he likes to spend most of his time with, and then with work and sports he's so busy it's hard for him to find time to study. He's smart, and my mom and dad really want him to go to college, so they're harder on him than they ever were on Josúe, and that makes him mad."

"And how are you doing?"

"I'm okay," she said in a way Brianne knew she really was. "I have this love for my mom that's different somehow. I used to get so mad at her, but I don't feel that way anymore. There are moments when I do, but then I pray, and I feel better."

Brianne didn't say anything. It was hard for her to imagine because Marissa's family was so different than hers, but she knew she could pray for them, and she was happy to listen to whatever Marissa wanted to share. Marissa added something else.

"One of the things that used to really bug me was my mom never came to any of my volleyball or basketball games or seemed interested in anything I was doing at school, except getting good grades. But now I'm happy to do those things for myself because I enjoy them instead of looking for her to be proud of me. And I know that's come from God because the week after I went to camp with you, I was feeling that way about our home volleyball game, and before I went out on the court, I heard this little voice say, 'Just have fun, Marissa. That's why you're doing this, not to gain her love. She already loves you, but she can't always show you in the ways you want.' Ever since then I've been a lot happier."

Brianne knew she had the opposite problem. Her parents showed her how much they loved her all the time, but she didn't always appreciate it. A memory flashed through her mind of a time last spring when she'd had a track meet. Her mom and dad had come like they always did, but her mom had forgotten to bring extra water like she'd asked her to. She had gotten mad and said something about how she never listened. The thought of it now made her feel awful.

She continued painting and had a fun time with Marissa and her other friends at Austin's house that evening, but when she got home, the memory of the way she had acted that day returned to her thoughts, and she knew it hadn't been the only time she had acted spoiled and selfish. Her mom had simply forgotten the water, and she couldn't think of a single time her parents had been unloving toward her or treated her unfairly or not taken care of her properly. She didn't always get her way, but it wasn't because they were being selfish or demanded too much from her.

She had arrived home at bedtime for her younger siblings, and she helped Beth with getting into her pajamas and brushing her teeth, and then when Beth wanted Mommy to tuck her in, she read a book to her until her mom was done in her brothers' room and came to say good night to Beth.

Brianne went into the living room where her dad was going over his message for tomorrow. When her mom joined them, she asked how her time had gone at the church this afternoon and at Austin's this evening.

"It was fun," she said. "Marissa's a really fast painter, so we did a room all by ourselves, and Pastor Doug was really impressed. He sent Austin, Jason, and Tim to help us when they finished with their room, but we were already done, and ours was bigger."

"How many kids were there?"

"About ten, I think."

"How's Marissa doing?"

"Good. She amazes me."

"Why?"

"Being home right now is hard, but she's smiling anyway. She said knowing God and going to Him is making a difference, but I don't think I could handle it as well as she does."

"God gives us what we need when we need it," her dad said, apparently listening to their conversation even though he was looking at his notes.

"I'm glad I don't need it," she said. A lump had hardened in her throat, and her voice came out shaky. She could picture the day she had gotten mad about the water as if it had happened yesterday. She hadn't thought about it at the time, but now she could see the reality of how badly she had acted. Her mom forgetting a water bottle was nothing compared to what Marissa had to face day after day.

"What's wrong, honey?" her mom asked. "Did something happen today? You sound upset."

"No, nothing happened," she said, moving closer to her mom and falling into her arms. She started crying fully then.

She cried and cried and felt her dad come sit on her other side, but her face was buried in her mom's shoulder. Once the tears stopped, her dad spoke.

"What is it, sweetheart?"

"I love you. I love both of you so much."

"We love you too," her mom said.

She sat back and took both of their hands. "I know you do, and I'm sorry I forget that sometimes. I'm sorry I get mad over stupid stuff and act like you're the worst parents ever, because you're not."

"That's good to know," her dad laughed.

She smiled and turned to hug him, holding on for a long time. "I love you, Daddy."

"I love you, sweetheart. Keep being who you are because we think you're pretty great too."

She hugged her mom also, without tears this time, although the lump in her throat was still there. She didn't confess the specific memory she had about the water because she knew there had been other times when she'd snapped at her mom for no good reason, and also because she knew her mom had already forgiven her for it long ago.

"I love you, Mama," she said simply instead.

"I love you too, baby. We're always here for you, for anything you need."

"I know."

She told them both good night and went to her room, knowing they could use some peace and quiet after a long day of being parents. She was up for another hour, writing a letter to Sarah, reading her Bible, and having an extra-long prayer time where she thanked God for her family and for reminding her how special they were. She confessed specific instances she could think of when she hadn't been a great daughter or sister, and she asked God to forgive her for those times and to help her avoid unnecessary moments like that in the future. She knew she wasn't perfect and there would be times she got frustrated or angry when things weren't going her way, but she asked God to help her change that.

She also prayed for Marissa and her family, for Silas' sister, and for Sarah, asking Jesus to give them exactly what they needed at this time in their lives. She wanted them to trust God and believe in His love for them like never before.

She prayed the same thing for herself, but she knew He had already given her everything she needed, and she felt so grateful. His love and the love all around her had become obvious today, and she didn't want to forget how truly blessed she was.

Chapter Seven

Monday was Veteran's Day, so Brianne didn't mail her letter to Joel until Tuesday, but she received one from him that same afternoon. It was mostly informative about what he had been doing the last few weeks, and he said how good it had been to see her and that he definitely hadn't forgotten about taking her up to his lookout tower. *Who do you think I built it for in the first place?* She didn't know if he was serious, but the thought of him doing so gave her a little thrill.

That Saturday she received another letter from him in response to her latest one. It wasn't long, but it was what she wanted to hear:

Dear Brianne,

I just got your second letter, and I'd like to say I agree with Silas about not wanting to see you end up like Danielle someday. And I'll add my own hopes that you become like my own sister. You're already a lot like Megan, and I know she would be there to talk if you ever need that, and I'm here for anything you need too. Thanks for caring enough to write and say you feel the same way about me. To be honest I have a difficult time connecting with people here—both guys and girls. Most of my friends are more into video games and skateboarding than going fishing and building lookout towers. And living here at the camp isolates me from them a lot too. As far as girls go, you're definitely the only one I would consider to be a friend. Most of them drive me crazy, and the others are more shy than me!

Joel

She saw him less than two weeks later. Her family drove to the camp the day after Thanksgiving. They stayed in the house that was part of the retreat center, and they were planning to stay until late Saturday afternoon. They spent most of Friday all together as two families who hadn't seen each other since this summer. It rained most of the day and snowed in the evening as it got colder.

On Saturday she was able to go for a walk through the fresh powder with Joel and his dog, Sam. It was a sunny day but cold. Because her family was going to her grandparents' for Christmas this year, they wouldn't be coming here like they sometimes did, and Joel surprised her by giving her an early Christmas present, something she hadn't thought of doing for him this soon.

"What's this?" she asked, taking the small wrapped package from him.

"It's a Christmas present."

"I can see that," she laughed. "I didn't get you anything."

"It's not Christmas yet."

"I know! Why are you giving me one now?"

"It's not the kind of thing I want to send you in the mail. When you wrote me and said that about having to trust in God's love above anyone else's, I went to the camp store and got this for you."

She took off the wrapping paper and opened the small box, not believing what she saw inside. He reached out and took the silver ring from its place and explained himself.

"I know a lot of guys get these for their girlfriends because it says LOVE on it, but I'm giving it to you for a different reason. I want you to wear it as a reminder that you are loved by God."

She took the band and slipped it onto her finger and smiled at him. "Thank you," she said, giving him a hug and holding on for a long time. She had a lot of good friends, but there was something very special about Joel. Maybe because she had known him the longest. But whatever the reason, she knew she missed him.

He held her gently and said, "You have to come work here someday. I want at least one whole summer with you here again."

"I will if you will," she said, stepping back and waiting for his response.

"I will."

"Promise?"

"I promise."

"And what about next summer? Are you going to be here the same week I am? Not just here, but as a camper?"

"Yes. Let me know when you're coming, and I'll sign up for that week too."

"Promise? I mean it. Last year was a major bummer without you here."

"I promise," he said.

**

On Sunday morning, Brianne witnessed a miracle happen right before her eyes. For the first time since Silas' family had moved here, Danielle was at church. She came in with Silas, and they sat next to her.

Danielle participated in worship and had tears on her cheeks during the last song. When Brianne went with the others to their class, Danielle stayed with the older students, but Silas didn't say anything about her being there until the class time was over. Apparently he didn't want to in front of everyone because he waited until it was just her and Austin left in the room. Both of them wanted to know why she was here and couldn't leave without asking.

"Mostly I think it's because of prayer, but my mom and dad were gone on Friday and yesterday. They went to the beach. That's the first time they've left us alone overnight because before Dani started having problems, she wasn't old enough, and since she has been, they haven't trusted her. But they asked her if she could be home this weekend, and she said yes, and yesterday afternoon she talked to her boyfriend in California, which she isn't supposed to do, but she did, and they ended up having this big fight with each other on the phone.

"Later I went and talked to her and told her things I've told her before about God loving her and not having to live like she is, and she kept telling me to go away. But then I asked her something. I said, 'Do you believe God still loves you, Dani?'

"She didn't answer me, so I just told her He did, and I also told her about what you had said, Brianne: about how even if others have hurt us, we can always trust that God won't. And I said, 'I know you don't want to go to church with me here because you feel like you can't trust anybody; and maybe you can't. But you can trust God, Dani. You can trust Him to get you out of this pit to a place of enjoying Him like you used to.'"

"And she listened?" Brianne asked.

"I didn't know if she did last night, but this morning she got up and got ready for church and came with me."

They could see the high school group was finishing up, so they left the room and Silas went to meet up with his sister. Brianne went to find her mom like she usually did to see if she needed her help with Children's Church. They had a schedule where different people helped on different weeks, but if someone who was supposed to be there couldn't make it, then she would fill in for them.

She told her mom about Danielle being here, and when her mom said she didn't need her help, Brianne went to the main church service and sat with Austin's family like she often did, along with Silas and Danielle who came in about ten minutes late with Pastor Doug. During one of the songs, Brianne noticed Danielle crying again, and she had tears on her cheeks often while her dad was giving the message for the morning, especially near the end when her dad said:

"It's not an accident you're on this earth. It's not an accident you're here this morning to hear a message about God's incredible love for you. You were created on purpose, for a purpose, and God wants so badly for you to discover that. And if you don't, He still loves you, but you're missing it. You're missing the life He has designed specifically for you."

On Monday morning when Silas came up the street to wait for the bus with her, he had a smile on his face that wouldn't go away. Brianne hadn't had a chance to talk with him any more yesterday. Austin's family often took Silas home on Sunday afternoons because his parents couldn't pick him up until later, so she asked him if anything else had happened.

"We went to Pastor Doug's house after church and had lunch with them, and Danielle talked to him and Mrs. Lockhart for a long time. After we went home, she told me she wants to get baptized again."

"When is she getting baptized?"

"Next Sunday."

"Silas! That's so cool," she said, giving him a hug. She heard the bus coming up the street, so she didn't hang on too long, not wanting to give anyone the wrong idea about them, but he seemed to appreciate her happiness.

Danielle was in high school, but she rode the same bus as them because they all attended the same campus. A new high school or middle school building was needed, but because of low school budgets they had to share for now and were on the same schedule. But even so, Danielle didn't normally ride the bus in the morning and only sometimes in the afternoon. She refused to get up early enough to catch it and made her mom drive her, and if her mom wouldn't then she just didn't go to school. In the afternoons she often went other places and didn't come home until well after dinnertime.

But as the bus approached Silas' house, Brianne saw Danielle waiting. It stopped for her and then came further up the street to pick up her and Silas also. Silas sat beside his sister, and Brianne sat in front of them. Danielle said 'hi' to her and handed her a small white envelope.

"Could you give that to your dad for me?"

"Sure," she said, taking the envelope from her and putting it in the front pouch of her backpack. Catching sight of the silver LOVE ring on her finger Joel had given to her on Saturday, she was reminded of a prayer she had whispered for herself and her friends, Beth and her brothers, and also for Danielle on Saturday night before she went to sleep.

Show us your love, Jesus. Remind us of it every day. And help us to see it.

She knew Danielle had been reminded of God's love for her, but she had seen it too. If He loved Danielle enough to go after her when she had been so lost, He wasn't going to ever stop loving her either.

Chapter Eight

Brianne knew she had a busy December ahead of her. Her mom and dad were going to be busy with things at church and she would need to watch after her siblings a lot, and she had her own activities too. Her class at school was putting together a winter play this year. It was a fun story about a teenage girl who wanted to go to the North Pole to meet one of Santa's grandsons who was rumored to be very cute and looking for a girlfriend. He was having a contest to bring a certain number of girls to the North Pole from all over the world. To enter the contest, the girl had to write an essay describing the way her family celebrated Christmas, or any other December holiday, and why she thought their way was the best.

Santa's granddaughter was having a similar contest, only she was looking for a boyfriend, and she was interested in boys who could sing or had some kind of special talent, so she was having a competition where the contestants had to sing a holiday song or perform something that was a popular way of celebrating the holidays in his country. The finalists would win a trip to the North Pole and have the chance to read their essay or perform for Santa and his grandchildren, and then whoever won would be able to travel the world on Christmas Eve with their new boyfriend or girlfriend and help deliver presents to all the children.

The twist in the story came when the boy and girl who were selected traveled with Santa's grandchildren to deliver the presents and discovered these particular grandchildren were very greedy and wanted to keep the best gifts for themselves rather than giving them away. So the winners of the contest stole the sleigh to do the job themselves and fell in love with each other.

The roles had been selected in early November, and Brianne had received a small role as the younger sister of one of the contestants who helps write her older sister's essay because her sister isn't a very good writer. They had been having rehearsals every Tuesday and Thursday for the last two weeks, except on Thanksgiving when there hadn't been any school, and they would be having rehearsals for the next two weeks, plus dress rehearsals before their performance.

Brianne had acted in small plays before for both school and church, and she always had fun, so she wasn't that nervous about it until she went to rehearsal on the first Tuesday in December and learned the girl who played her big sister couldn't play the part after all because she had a dance recital on the same night as the play.

Since Brianne already knew a lot of her lines because she had been playing opposite her, Mrs. Murphey asked if she would take the more prominent role, and they would find someone else to do her part.

Brianne knew she could do it, but she'd never had such a big part in anything before, and when she got home later, she panicked.

"Mom! I can't do it. Why did I say yes?"

"Yes, you can, honey. You're a great actress, and you memorize so easily."

"But Emma has a bunch of lines in the second part of the play after she goes to the North Pole that I haven't even looked at yet, and the play is in two weeks!"

"You can do it, honey," she repeated. "Your dad and I will help you, and I'm sure Austin will too. He's in the play, isn't he?"

She laughed. "Yes, he's the guy who wins his way into the finals by telling a version of *T'was The Night Before Christmas* with some very flattering lines for Santa's beautiful granddaughter. It's really funny."

"You should ask him to rehearse with you on Saturday or after school."

"Okay," she said, knowing she could use Austin's help. "And we could probably practice on our way to our classes every day too."

"How's that been going?" her mom asked.

"What?"

"Having Austin in all of your classes and seeing him all day long."

"Fine," she said honestly. "At first it felt weird, but now we're both used to it, and I don't think about it most of the time. He's just always there."

"How's he been doing with Sarah being away?"

"Okay. They've been writing to each other, but I don't think anything is really happening. At least neither of them have said anything to me."

Her words were confirmed when she received a letter from Sarah the following day. At first she couldn't believe what she was reading, but Sarah did a thorough job of explaining herself.

Dear Brianne,

I have something to tell you that I don't know if you'll agree with or not, but I know I can't keep it from you, and I hope you won't be too mad at me. Just hear me out, okay?

On Sunday Ryan and I had a long talk. As I told you before, we decided to try the church his family has been going to the last several weeks, and we like it too. We've been going on Sundays, and Scott and I have been going to youth group on Sunday nights plus to a more focused Bible-study thing they have on Wednesdays, and we love it. Mom and Dad like the church too, and so do Ryan and his family, so it looks like we're all going to be attending there.

Anyway, on Sunday night after youth group, we went Christmas caroling for an hour around the streets surrounding the church, and Ryan had something he wanted to ask me. He asked me if I wanted to be his girlfriend, and I said yes.

Now, before you freak out on me, let me explain. We're not going to date. His parents

74

won't let him do that yet, and he doesn't feel ready for it anyway. And we're also not going to kiss because I told him I don't feel ready for that kind of a relationship yet, and he said he doesn't either. But we are going to be more than friends, and I can't explain why, but as we were talking and telling each other what we both want and don't want our relationship to be like, I felt okay with it. Like God was telling me it's okay to have a "boyfriend" right now if that boyfriend is Ryan.

He is so sweet, Brianne. He sort of reminds me of Austin. When he first asked me to be his girlfriend, I immediately said 'no' and gave him all my reasons why. I told him about what had happened with Brady, and he said, 'If you're my girlfriend, then you'll have the perfect excuse for telling guys like that to buzz off.' And I don't know what it was, but I believed his intentions were genuine, and I really liked the thought of having a guy like Ryan to sort of protect me, I guess.

So, I'm going to give it a try, and who knows, maybe by next week I'll be writing you another letter that says, 'That was the stupidest idea ever!' But I told God I'm trusting Him with the details and to feel free to get me out of this if it's a mistake, but the time I spent with Ryan today tells me it isn't. I want you to meet him. Do you think you can visit me sometime before Christmas Break? I know you're busy, but if you can make it work, I'd love to see you.

I know you're thinking, 'What about Austin? How can you do this to him?' I'm writing him a letter too, and I hope he understands, but if he seems down at school tomorrow, you'll know why. I know it's a lot to ask, but can you talk to him? It's not about me choosing Ryan over him, it's about Austin being there and Ryan being here, and I could really use a friend like him right now. He's the only person I've really connected with in the last three months. There are a couple of girls at church I'm getting to know, but they don't go to my school. This might sound weird, but I feel like Ryan is to me here what you were to me there. Do you remember how we were right from the start? How everything was so easy and perfect and we didn't have to work at being best friends, it just happened? Well, that's how I feel about Ryan. Like I found a best friend here, but he happens to be a boy. Please don't hate me. I'll keep you posted about how it's going, and let me know if you can come for a visit soon.

Miss you,
Sarah

This I declare of the LORD: 'He alone is my refuge, my place of safety. He is my God, and I am trusting him!' Psalm 91:2

Brianne knew she needed that verse for herself because she had already arranged to go to Austin's house tonight after dinner so they could work on their lines for the play together. She wasn't going to see Austin's reaction to this news tomorrow, she would be seeing it in a few hours.

She had mixed feelings about Sarah's words. In a way she felt mad at Sarah for breaking the promise they had made to each other about not dating until they were sixteen, but technically she wasn't dating Ryan, she was just his girlfriend, so she hadn't gone back on her word, at least not yet. Brianne felt skeptical that Sarah could be Ryan's girlfriend for long before it turned into something where they did start going out with each other and kissing.

But she also knew Sarah well enough to believe she wasn't compromising anything. Having a best friend who was a boy was something Brianne could see Sarah handling just fine, and if Ryan was as nice as Sarah said, she was happy she had made a good friend. She had been praying for that for the past three months, especially since she had gone to see her at the beginning of October and saw how lonely she was.

But her heart broke for Austin. He was a nice guy too, and his only fault was he lived an hour and a half away now instead of in the same neighborhood. He had pursued something with Sarah while she'd been here, but she had resisted him. Why was she okay with it now with a guy she had only known for two months?

"Are you okay, honey?" her mom asked while she was helping her make dinner.

Brianne hadn't said anything about the letter to her mom, mainly because she wasn't sure how she felt about it. One minute she was fine, and the next she felt like she was losing Sarah as her best friend. What if Sarah didn't have time to write to her anymore because she spent so much time with Ryan and told him everything instead of her? What if she lost interest in having her as a friend and they never had times like they used to ever again? What if she went to visit her sometime this month and she met Ryan and didn't like him? Would she have the courage to tell Sarah she thought she was making a huge mistake, and would that be her place?

She told her mom about the letter and everything Sarah had said about Ryan and the relationship they were going to have. When she finished, her mom asked how she felt about it.

"I'm mad!" she admitted, tossing aside the spoon she had used to stir the meat sauce for the tacos.

"Why?"

Brianne sighed. "I don't know. I just am."

"Are you mad at Sarah?"

"No, not really."

"Are you mad at God?"

She knew that was it, but she didn't say those exact words. "It's not supposed to be like this." She started crying, and her mom turned to hug her. "Why did she have to move? I don't understand."

Her mom didn't say anything and let her cry. When she stopped, her mom kept holding her gently and said, "God has reasons we don't know about, Bree. But I promise they're good reasons. We can always count on that, even when it doesn't seem like it."

Chapter Nine

After dinner Brianne's dad drove her to Austin's house as planned. She hadn't said anything to her dad about Sarah, and she kept it to herself on the drive. What her mom had said about God's plans being for the best helped her think about it differently and not be so upset, but she didn't know if Austin would see it that way. She had no idea what she was going to say to him.

When she arrived, Austin's mom welcomed her at the door, and she went inside the spacious home Pastor Doug had finished building last year, replacing the older mobile home they had lived in before. It had a main living room, a large kitchen and dining room, four bedrooms, and another family room area with a view of the Columbia River.

"Austin is in the other room if you want to go on back," Mrs. Lockhart said.

"Thanks," she replied.

She saw Austin practicing his guitar beside the large window. He played drums in band and at church, and he had been taking private lessons to learn guitar.

He looked up when she came into the room, and he didn't appear disturbed. He put his guitar on its stand and got up from the chair, seeming to be as he always was: casual and emotionless. "I thought we could practice in here. Is that all right?"

"Yeah, that's fine," she said.

He took his script from the top of the piano and sat in one of the more comfortable chairs in the large room. Brianne took the small sofa, but she waited for Austin to speak.

"Where should we start?" he asked.

The script was the furthest thing from her mind, and she decided to go ahead and say it. "How about with Sarah?"

He didn't take his eyes from the paper. "Where's that?"

"Not Sarah in the play. I mean Sarah, Sarah."

"Huh?"

"Sarah Anderson? Did you get a letter from her today?"

"Yeah," he said, but not with the emotion she was expecting. "What's there to talk about?"

"I don't know. How do you feel about it?"

He shrugged. "She sounds happy."

"You're not mad?"

He laughed. "It's not like I was expecting her to be my girlfriend now that she's moved. She didn't want to be when she was here."

"But she's been writing to you."

"They haven't been love letters."

"Has she said anything to you about Ryan before now?"

"Yep, she talked about him a lot. I wasn't surprised."

"So, you're okay with it?"

"Sure."

She stared at him, trying to determine if he was being straight with her or hiding his disappointment well.

He laughed. "Honestly, I'm fine, Brianne. Come on, we've got lines to memorize."

She turned her eyes to her script and decided to let Austin practice his part first. Her mind wasn't fully focused on the play yet. Austin had everything down except his story he was supposed to recite.

"I can work on that more on my own," he said. "Do you want a snack before we go to your part?"

"Sure."

They went to the kitchen, and his mom pointed out some things they could have. Austin decided he wanted a sandwich and began making himself one. She said she was fine with chips and juice.

"You would think he didn't have dinner," Mrs. Lockhart said to her. "I've heard other moms talk about teenage boys cleaning out the refrigerator, and now I know why."

Brianne noticed Austin had gotten taller since this summer when he'd had a good growth spurt. Before that they had been even in height, but he was at least two inches taller than her now. And since his dad was about six-two, she knew he wouldn't be stopping anytime soon.

"He tries to steal food from me at lunch every day," she said. "And Brooke too. She usually gives him half of her sandwich or grabs pizza for him when she has hot lunch."

"Austin!" his mom laughed. "People are going to think I never feed you."

He stepped over to his mom and stood nose to nose with her. They were the exact same height now, and his mom wasn't short. "I don't think they'll think that," he said.

She kissed him on the forehead and pushed him away. "I knew this day would come, I just can't believe it came this soon."

Taking their snacks into the other room, Brianne set hers on the table at the end of the sofa and Austin kept his full plate on his lap. "Okay, your turn," he said. "Where should we start?"

She found the first page where her character speaks and began there. She had most of those lines down pretty well, and it helped her get into character before moving on to the new scenes. She had practiced them today, and she was surprised she remembered as much as she did.

"You're a good actress, Brianne," Austin said after they had gone over the new portion several times.

"Thanks," she said. "I like it. It's fun."

"You're good at making me believe you could actually be Emma, even though I know you would never be like that."

"Like what?"

"Snotty and spoiled. Girls like that drive me crazy. I'm glad you're not."

"Does that mean you're not tired of me yet? After three months of us having all of our classes together?"

"No. I'm not." He hesitated and then added. "In a way I feel like we're becoming best friends, don't you?"

She thought about that and smiled. "Yeah, I guess so." She had made some new friends this year with Brooke and Silas, and she had strengthened others with Emily and Marissa, but if she had to pick one person as her best friend besides Sarah, it would be Austin.

"Are you going to keep writing to Sarah?" she asked, seriously wanting to know.

"Yes. Just because she has Ryan now doesn't mean she doesn't still need us."

"How long do you think the no-dating and no-kissing thing will last?"

He smiled. "If it was me, it wouldn't last too long, but maybe Ryan can handle it."

"I think it's kind of a cool idea. I was shocked at first, but I can see Sarah doing something like that. It makes good sense for her."

"Would you ever do something like that, or are you still waiting until you're sixteen?"

She thought for a moment. Originally the 'waiting until sixteen' thing had been because that's what Sarah was going to do, but the idea had become her own over the last three months, and she felt like she wanted to stick with it.

"I'm waiting," she said.

"I hope you do."

"Why?"

"I like the idea of us being best friends for the next few years. I'm not sure you having a boyfriend would fit into that."

"Or you having a girlfriend," she added.

He smiled. "I won't if you won't."

"Seriously?"

"Sure."

She laughed. "Is that a promise?"

"No, not a promise. More like a pact."

"A pact?"

"Yeah, like if either of us decide we want to change our mind before then, the other person has to agree they're making a good decision. As your best friend, I have a right to tell you what I think, and you have to listen; and the same goes for me."

"The last time I made a pact with someone, it didn't last too long."

"But Sarah would take anything you have to say seriously. If you wrote her back and told her you think this is a mistake, she would listen to you."

She laughed. "Is that what you want me to do?"

He laughed too but answered seriously. "No. I'm not saying it's a mistake. I don't think you feel that way either, but if you did, she would value your opinion and advice. Don't you think?"

"Yes. I guess so," she agreed. "And you would too? You would listen to me if I said, 'I don't think you should date—whoever'?"

"I could still make my own choice, but I'd listen, unless—"

"Unless what?" she asked.

"Never mind."

"Austin! What were you going to say? Best friends tell each other everything."

He looked embarrassed, but he finished his thought. "Unless the reason you tell me no is out of jealousy."

"Jealousy?"

"It has to be about what's best for the other person, not yourself."

"You mean like if I don't want to lose you as a best friend?"

"Yeah that, or—"

She smiled. "Or if I want you for myself?"

He turned red.

She laughed. "Honestly, Austin. I don't think you need to worry about that. I think you're great, but I can't really picture us—you know. But I do like the thought of you watching out for me, so don't be afraid to tell me what you really think."

He smiled. "Remember who said that."

Austin's dad came into the room and asked if they were finished. He had already said he would drive her home around this time.

"Yeah, we're done," she said, getting up from the sofa and grabbing her script. She said good night to Austin and his mom as she followed Pastor Doug out the front door. After they were in the truck and on the road, heading toward her house a short distance away, her youth pastor brought up the subject of Silas' sister, asking what she had heard from Silas.

"She broke up with her boyfriend and got rid of a bunch of stuff—music and clothes and posters and whatever else she had in her room and on her phone; Silas says she's back to being the sister he used to know in a lot of ways, but not completely yet. He hopes she can get there."

"Did you ever know Janie Weber? Or was she gone before you moved here?"

"Mr. and Mrs. Weber's daughter?"

"Yes."

"I've never met her, but I've heard a little bit from my dad. Why?"

"Similar story as Danielle, except she didn't go her own way until her senior year, but it shocked me like Danielle's choices surprised Silas and his family."

Brianne had a feeling she knew where Pastor Doug was going with this, and she wanted to say that wasn't going to happen to her, but she supposed Danielle and Janie never thought it would happen to them either.

"You remind me of Janie," he said, confirming her thoughts. "Before things went sour, anyway. And after talking with Danielle and hearing how ashamed she felt about her choices that kept her from getting the help she needed, I want you to know I'm here for you, Brianne. No matter what, you can always come to me, okay? That's what I'm here for."

"Okay," she said and added something based on what she and Austin had been talking about. "And I give you permission to tell me whatever you think about the choices I make. And if that doesn't work, send Austin. He can be really honest when he wants to be."

He laughed. "You're good for him, Brianne. Keep an eye on him for me, okay?"

She smiled. "Yes, I'll do that. And if he's not listening to you, send me."

Chapter Ten

"Where did you get that ring?"

Brianne looked up from the mixture she was stirring for their chemistry experiment and decided to tease Austin. After their conversation last night and the little pact they'd made, she knew it was perfect timing.

"From a boy."

"Who?"

She laughed. "Joel."

"Joel? He bought you a ring that says LOVE?"

"Yep."

He didn't say anything, and she laughed again.

"Are you jealous, Austin Lockhart?"

"No."

"Liar."

"I'm not jealous. I'm just wondering."

She told him the truth. "He gave it to me as an early Christmas present, and it doesn't mean anything—at least not between me and him. He gave it to me because I had written him a letter about what Silas said to me about Danielle, and I wanted him to know I'm here for him as a friend too, and then when we went there, he gave me the ring to wear as a reminder that God loves me."

"Why do I have the feeling he's the guy I'm going to have to say, 'Okay, you can date him.'?"

"Me and Joel?" She laughed. "I don't think so."

"Why not?"

"He's like my cousin or something. Even more than you."

Austin let it go, but the thought remained with her for the rest of the class period. The truth was she had thought about Joel in that way in the past, especially this summer when he wasn't at camp for part of the week and she realized how much she missed him, but it hadn't lasted. She had been too caught up with Sarah moving away and starting seventh grade without her.

When she got home from school, she decided to write to him again, thanking him for the ring and letting him know how often she had been reminded God loved her by looking at it off and on throughout the day. She also told him the good news about Danielle, and she asked him to pray for Janie, the girl Pastor Doug had mentioned last night.

On Friday afternoon her dad drove her to Portland to see Sarah. Sarah's birthday was on Saturday, and after looking at the calendar for this month, they had decided this would be the best time to go visit her. Next weekend they had a dress rehearsal for the play, and the following weekend her parents were putting on a Christmas dinner at church and they would be getting ready to go to Washington for Christmas.

Because of both of their parents' schedules this weekend, Sunday afternoon would be the best time for Sarah's mom to bring her back, so she was excited about staying two nights this time. Sarah had plans for her to meet Ryan at her birthday party, and she would probably see him on Sunday too, but otherwise it would be just her and Sarah. They watched two movies on Friday night before they went to bed, and they stayed up late talking like old times. Sarah told her more about Ryan and what her week had been like as his girlfriend, saying it hadn't been different from just being friends except they spent a little more time together.

"He's really nice, Brianne. He reminds me of Austin as a guy, but he's also a lot like you. We have a lot of fun together just goofing around, and I feel like I can tell him anything."

Brianne smiled. She had never seen Sarah like this before. She was the same, but different. And it was a good different.

In return Brianne told her about Silas and Danielle, her time with Joel, and her conversation with Austin on Wednesday night. Sarah smiled when she told her about the pact they had agreed on.

"I've been praying for that, Bree."

"For what?"

"For Austin to decide to wait instead of going after another girl now that I'm gone."

"Why?"

"I don't know. I'd hate to see Austin get caught up in all of that right now. I think it's great he has a friend like you to keep him grounded. He's more easily influenced by his peers than you."

"I think he's changed since last year. His time at camp this summer was a turning point for him. Did I ever tell you what he told me on the last day?"

"I don't think so."

"We talked about what it's like to have dads who are pastors, and we both agreed it can be hard sometimes, but basically we're okay with it."

"Okay with it? You two have the most awesome dads I've ever met!"

"Yeah, but it's not always easy to see that when you're their kid."

"I suppose so."

"How are your mom and dad taking this thing with you and Ryan?"

"Fine, I guess. They didn't really say anything when I told them. My mom was like, 'That's nice, honey,' and my dad didn't speak."

"Do they like him?"

"Yeah, they like him. But, I don't know, I feel like they don't care about what I do right now."

"What makes you think that?"

"They're busy. My dad works late almost every night, and my mom's doing a million different things. It's weird. Ever since we moved here, it's like we're living a different family's life. We're closer in some ways, but—"

"I'm sure they care, Sarah. They trust you to make good choices."

"Yeah, I guess."

"What would you do if they said you couldn't have a boyfriend yet?"

"I think I'd listen and tell Ryan we should wait, and I think he would be fine with that, especially if that's what my mom and dad wanted."

Brianne asked her next question more cautiously. "What would you do if I told you *I* was concerned and you shouldn't be doing this?"

Sarah took her question seriously. "Are you telling me that?"

"No. I'm just wondering."

"I have always listened to you, Brianne. Do you think I'm making a mistake? Honestly?"

"I think I need to meet Ryan first. From everything you've told me, I think it's fine. But I need to see it for myself, you know?"

"Yes, I know. And that's why I wanted you to meet him. I feel like I'm on my own so much here. I haven't gotten to know the youth pastor at church well enough to feel like he's looking out for me like Pastor Doug would be right now. And even your mom and dad have been like second parents to me, but they're not living next door anymore. I need you to do this for me, Brianne. I think I'm hearing God fine, but maybe I'm not. Please be honest with me about this, okay?"

"Okay. I can do that."

***

In the morning they went to the store with Sarah's mom to get things for her party that afternoon. Sarah had only invited Ryan, two girls from church, and a couple of girls from school. Everyone she had invited said they were coming, and they were planning to open gifts and eat cake at the house and then go ice skating at a nearby rink.

Her mom bought a cake instead of making one like she had done in the past, and Brianne could see what Sarah meant about her mom being a lot more busy and distracted here. In Clatskanie Sarah's mom hadn't worked an outside job except for doing some volunteer hours as the church secretary. But since they had moved here, she had been working full-time as a receptionist for a doctor's office, and her mom didn't get home until five every day.

During volleyball season, Sarah hadn't noticed the difference so much because she didn't usually get home until later too, but now that she was home more, it seemed strange to not have her mom there when she got home from school. Ryan's mom was usually home in the afternoon, along with his two younger brothers and a sister, so Sarah had gone there several days this week.

Ryan arrived fifteen minutes early. Sarah had asked him to so they could meet each other, and Brianne thought he seemed nice. He was very cute: similar to Brady but without the attitude. And although he remained close to Sarah's side throughout the party, Brianne didn't feel like he was intruding on her space as Sarah's best friend.

All of Sarah's friends seemed nice, and they had a lot of fun ice skating together. She talked with several of the girls when Sarah was skating with Ryan, and they all said similar things about Sarah being sweet and she and Ryan making the perfect couple.

After they returned to the house, Ryan stayed later than the others, but not that long. Before he left, he spoke to her and said, "I hope you don't hate me too much."

Brianne smiled. "I don't hate you. I'm jealous you get to see her every day, but I'm glad she's found a good friend here."

"And I'm glad I found her," he said, reaching for Sarah's hand. "But I'll go now so you can have her all to yourself."

"Bye, Ryan. It was nice meeting you."

Sarah walked him to the front door, and Brianne remained behind to give them privacy, but Sarah wasn't gone long, and when she returned, she asked what she wanted to do for the rest of the day.

"Could we go shopping? My mom gave me money to buy some Christmas presents."

"Sure. I'll see if my mom can drive us over."

Sarah went to ask her mom, and Brianne went to Sarah's room to get her money. While she was in there she remembered something else she had for Sarah besides the birthday present she had already given her during the party.

"My mom said it's fine if we want to go," Sarah said, coming into the room and heading for a decorative jar on her desk where she kept her spending money. "She has things to get too, so she'll go with us. Is that all right?"

"Yeah, that's fine," she said, holding out the sack to her she had taken out of her bag. "I have something else for you."

"What's this?"

"It's a birthday present, but I wanted to give it to you when it was just us."

Sarah opened the sack and took out the devotional book matching the one her dad had given to her back in September after she told him about wanting to read her Bible more and getting to know God in a more personal way.

"Is this the same one you have?" Sarah asked.

"Yes. I really like it, and I think you will too."

"Thanks," she said, stepping over to give her a hug. "I need something good right now." She stepped back and added, "I feel right about what's happening between me and Ryan, but at the same time I don't have a clue what I'm doing and I need God to show me."

"I'm sure He will," she said.

"Do you like him, Brianne, honestly? Do you think I'm making a mistake?"

"No, I don't think you are, and yes, I do like him. He actually reminds me a lot of my friend Joel, only he's more social like Austin."

"He was nervous about meeting you."

Brianne laughed. "Me? Why?"

"Because he knows how close we are and how much I value your opinion. When he left, he said, 'Do you think I passed, or should I ask for a good-bye kiss now?'"

"Tell him he passed, so no kisses!"

Sarah laughed and set the book on her desk. They left the room and headed downstairs, and they had a really fun time shopping. Brianne was mostly looking for things for her family, but she also wanted to get Joel something she could send to him.

Sarah was looking for something to get Ryan, and she had a couple of ideas. He liked to play video games, and he also liked to listen to music. But Brianne wasn't sure what to get for Joel. Sarah decided to get Ryan a music gift card and a frame to put a picture of herself in, and she suggested she do the same for Joel.

Brianne laughed. "I don't think he would want a picture of me."

"Sure, he would." She reached for a frame that had multiple openings. "Don't you have pictures of when you were kids? You could put some of those in these three and then one of just you. Your school picture was really nice this year."

Brianne wasn't too sure. "I'll think about it," she said, knowing she could get a frame back home if she decided she wanted to do that, but at this point she didn't think so.

Chapter Eleven

"Cute skirt," Sarah said. "When did you get that?"

Brianne took her plain white tennis shoes out of her bag she thought looked good with the pink denim skirt and sat down to put them on. "I got it in Sweet Home at a secondhand clothing store," she said. "I went shopping with my mom, Mrs. West, and Megan when we were there, and my mom found it on a rack and showed me. It was a little big in the waist, so she made it smaller."

"You always find the cutest stuff when you go to places like that."

"And at garage sales," she said.

"I bet people have a ton of them around here in the summer. You'll have to stay with me for a whole week sometime."

"Seriously? I'd love that."

"Sure. And maybe I can come for a week with you too."

"Are you planning to go to camp next summer?"

"I think so. Maybe Ryan can go. Or would you not like that?"

"Fine with me," she said.

"Do you think that would bother Austin?"

"I don't know. He seemed fine with you meeting someone when I talked to him about it."

Brianne liked the church they went to, and being there with Sarah reminded her of when they had first moved to Clatskanie and Sarah made a point to introduce her to all of her friends. She sat beside Sarah in the large room where the middle school students met, and there were about five times as many as they had in their entire youth group. Ryan sat beside Sarah there and in the large worship service that followed. If this church was a lot smaller than the one they had gone to before, she couldn't imagine how big it had been.

Brianne noticed Ryan holding Sarah's hand during the pastor's message like he had several times yesterday. Brianne tried to imagine what it would be like to have Silas holding her hand during church or while walking down the hall at school like she had seen other couples do, but she couldn't really picture it. She didn't feel ready for that, and she didn't feel like she needed it either. She thought it was fine for Sarah if that's what she wanted, but she didn't want it too just because Sarah did.

After church Brianne went with Sarah and her family out to lunch and then Sarah's mom drove her back to Clatskanie. Saying good-bye to Sarah wasn't easy, but she'd had a really fun weekend. She slept well after being up late on Friday and Saturday, and getting on the bus in the morning with Silas and Danielle and then seeing Austin a few minutes later made her realize she had missed seeing them at church yesterday. They asked how her weekend had gone, and she spoke in general terms with them and her other friends as the day went on, but she spoke more specifically about Sarah to Austin on their way to P.E. that afternoon.

"Ryan is nice. You would like him."

"Is he better looking than me?"

Brianne laughed. "I'm not answering that."

"Oh, come on. It's okay. I can take it."

Brianne hadn't really thought about it, and it was a hard judgment to make because Ryan and Austin were different. She supposed if she met both of them at the same time and didn't know them, she would see Ryan as being cuter because she tended to be initially attracted to that kind of look, but since she knew Austin as well as she did and had known him much longer, she honestly couldn't make a definite decision. They were both cute in their own way.

"I took some pictures of them at her birthday party. My mom was going to take them in to get some copies for me today, so you can see for yourself tomorrow."

"He's cuter," he said. "Just say it and spare me the pictures."

"He's not," she said, wondering why she felt the need to say that. "He's different than you."

"Better different?"

She punched him in the arm and laughed. "Stop it! You're just different."

"Like you and Sarah are different?"

His words stung. She knew Sarah was prettier than her, and hearing Austin point that out affected her more deeply than she was prepared for. She didn't respond and was glad they were almost to the entrance to the girls' locker room so she could escape this conversation.

"Okay, I can accept that," he said, seeming oblivious to her hurt feelings. "If I had to pick who was prettier between you and Sarah, I'd have a hard time too."

"That's not funny, Austin," she said, feeling unusually bold. "Thanks for hurting my feelings when I was being so careful not to hurt yours."

She turned away to go into the locker room, and he didn't stop her. Bypassing her locker, she went to the bathroom area, entered one of the empty stalls, and sat down to have a private cry over it.

Austin's reminder she wasn't as pretty as Sarah took her back to last year when boys had started asking Sarah out and yet none of them even glanced her way. It hadn't bothered her so much this year because she knew it hadn't been a great experience for Sarah, and none of her other close friends had boyfriends right now, but having Austin point out the major difference between her and Sarah just hurt. She couldn't believe he said that.

She didn't cry for very long, but she didn't want to face Austin right now so she went to Miss Lowe's office and told her she wasn't feeling well. Her crying had made her look flushed, so Miss Lowe let her go to the nurse, but she had to lie to the nurse when she asked her more specifically what was wrong. She told her she was having bad cramps from her period, which wasn't true, but the nurse didn't question it.

She had her lie on one of the beds, and she offered to call her mom to have her come pick her up, but she said she would be okay. Lying to the nurse was one thing. Lying to her mom would be much worse and harder to hide because she wasn't really having her period, and then she would have to explain why she hadn't wanted to go to P.E. today.

Lying there in the quiet room, Brianne wasn't sure why she had reacted so strongly to Austin's comment. She had certainly known before today that boys were more attracted to Sarah than her, and Austin was among them. But there was something about hearing him say the truth out loud that made it harder to deal with, especially since Sarah wasn't here anymore. She could never compete with that.

When the bell rang, she left the nurse's office and went to her locker to get the books she needed to take home tonight. She and Austin usually walked from the gym together, split to go to their individual lockers, and then met up again to walk to the bus, but she didn't wait for him today.

Taking an empty seat on the bus in their usual place, she didn't want to face him right now, but she knew he would be coming any minute. She took a book out of her bag she had gotten from Sarah this weekend and started reading it. Sarah bought lots of books and had always passed ones on to her she particularly liked, and this was the first in a series.

When Austin didn't get on the bus right away and it was getting pretty full, she knew he must be waiting for her inside because they usually got on before now. She thought about going to look for him but decided against it. They could both end up missing the bus, and they lived too far outside of town to walk home.

He finally arrived and took his usual seat beside her. She tried to act like nothing had happened and kept reading her book, but her mind wasn't focused on what she was reading.

"Brianne?"

"What?" she asked without looking up.

He took the book from her hands. She looked at him and saw an expression on his face she had never seen before.

"What happened to you? Why weren't you in P.E.?"

"I didn't feel good and went to the nurse."

"You were fine."

She didn't respond and reached for her book, but he wouldn't give it to her.

"Brianne, what's going on? I feel like I missed something."

"Can I have my book back, please?"

"No. Not until you talk to me."

"There's nothing to say. It doesn't matter."

"What doesn't matter? One minute you were telling me about Ryan and the next you were mad about something."

She snatched the book out of his hands and whispered it loudly. "You hurt my feelings, okay? I know Sarah is prettier than me, but you didn't have to say it."

"I didn't say that."

"Yes, you did!"

"No, I didn't."

His words were still fresh in her mind, and she repeated them back to him in a mocking tone of voice. "If I had to pick who was prettier between you and Sarah, I'd have a hard time too."

"I would," he defended.

"Austin, you're a bad liar. It's okay. I'm over it. Just forget—"

"I'm not lying. You're pretty. Sarah's pretty. You're just different. Like what you were saying about me and Ryan. Or were you lying to me about that?"

"No."

"So how is that any different than what I said to you?"

"Because I was being serious."

"So was I."

"Austin, just forget it," she said, opening her book and letting her eyes fall on the page. She expected Austin to leave her alone. They never argued. Not about serious stuff.

He did leave her alone for a minute, but the silence was uncomfortable. She tried to read her book, but she couldn't concentrate. She wondered if Austin was being honest or if he was trying to spare her feelings. He couldn't possibly see her and Sarah as equally pretty. He was lying, but at least he was making the effort. She decided she didn't want to throw their friendship away over it.

"I'm sorry," she said. She looked over at him, and he looked back. "Forgive me for having a girl-moment?"

"What's that?"

"When I get mad at you for being honest about how you feel about other girls. A friend would listen and accept it. But I took it too personally, so I'm sorry."

She felt better and started to turn back to her book, but his words stopped her.

"I don't get why you were mad in the first place."

She was getting annoyed. "Austin!"

"What? If I said something hurtful, I'd apologize, but I didn't."

"You don't think Sarah is prettier than me?" she challenged him.

"No. I think you're different."

"How are we different?"

"Okay, now you're having a girl-moment. I'm not going there."

She went back to her reading, and he sat there for a moment before he took out his iPod and listened to music the rest of the way to her stop. She said good-bye to him, and he did the same. Once she was off the bus, Danielle started walking down the street, but Silas hung back to talk to her.

"What's going on with you and Austin? It sounded like you were fighting. Are you okay?"

"Yeah, I'm fine," she said, knowing her words didn't sound too convincing.

"Do you want to talk about it?"

"No. It's no big deal. I'll see you tomorrow."

"Okay, but if you want to talk later, I live right over there."

She smiled. "I know. Thanks."

He let her go, and she walked slowly up the driveway, carrying the mail with her. There weren't any letters for her today, just bills and junk mail. Her mom was on the phone when she entered the house, so she left the mail on the counter and went to her room to put her backpack away and saw that Beth was still napping, so she went to the living room to read.

Listening to her mom talk, she figured out it was her grandmother on the phone. They were talking about the sleeping arrangements at the house. Some of her aunts, uncles, and cousins were going to be there too. It sounded like they were going to be staying in a motel part of the time, which they had done before when there were too many relatives to fit in the house all at once.

Brianne wished they were going tomorrow, that she didn't have to be in the play next week, or see Austin for a month. She felt stupid, embarrassed, and hurt.

When her mom got off the phone and came to ask about her day, she acted like everything was just peachy, and her mom didn't question it because she usually came home from school in a good mood. Her mom told her what they were thinking for the sleeping arrangements while they were in Washington. There were three nights around Christmas when everyone was going to be there, and those were the nights Grandma and Grandpa were going to pay for a hotel room for part of their family to stay in.

"Would you rather stay with us and Beth at the motel, or have Beth with you at Grandma's and we'll take the boys?"

"It doesn't matter to me," she said. "Whatever Beth wants."

"We'll probably decide after we're there. I think Beth is getting a cold. I hope she gets over it before we go."

The phone rang and her mom got up to answer it. She didn't talk very long to whomever it was, but she thanked the person for calling and then came to sit beside her again.

"That was the school nurse. She said you weren't feeling well today. Are you getting sick too, honey?"

Chapter Twelve

Brianne's mom laid her hand on her forehead and touched her cheeks with the back of her hand. "You don't feel warm," she said. "Does your throat hurt?"

Brianne didn't know what to say. She didn't want to lie to her mom like she had lied to the nurse, but she didn't know how to tell the truth without letting her mom know what had happened with Austin.

"No," she said. "I'm okay. It was during P.E. I didn't feel like going."

"Oh. Is it that time of the month?"

"No."

"So, you're fine?"

"Yeah. I feel better now."

Beth came into the room with her blanket and dolly in her arms, saving her from any more questions. Brianne laid down her book and pulled her little sister onto her lap. Beth laid her head on her chest. Her nose was running, so her mom got up to get her some tissue and then took her temperature. It was only at 100, so her mom left her alone and went to get her juice.

Brianne sat there holding Beth, read some of her books, and then laid down on the couch with her while they watched an episode of *Little Bear* on TV. When that was over, Beth got down to play and Brianne went to her room to get her backpack and start on her homework. She had just finished her math when her brothers came home from school and she had to retreat to her room if she wanted peace and quiet.

"Are you going over to Austin's tonight?" her mom asked before she stepped out of the room.

Brianne froze. She had forgotten about their plans to practice their lines together for the play. They had talked about it last week, and she had planned to ask him on the way home if he still wanted to, but she had forgotten about it until now.

"I forgot to ask him," she said.

If this had been a normal day, she would have gone to the phone and called him, and she knew her mom was waiting for her to say she would, but she didn't want to. She did need to practice her lines. She hadn't much this weekend, but she didn't know if she could face him.

"What's wrong, honey? You haven't been yourself since you got home. Are you sure you're feeling okay?"

She looked away, not wanting to lie but not knowing how to answer that. Physically she felt fine, but emotionally—she wasn't sure how she felt. She hated having unresolved issues with her friends, and she really hated it with Austin.

It was all too much and she burst into tears. Without saying anything, her mom stepped over and steered her away from the living room. They went to her room where they could have privacy.

"What happened, honey?" her mom asked, sitting down on the bed beside her. "Did something happen with Austin today?"

"Yes."

"What?"

"I had a girl-moment."

Her mom laughed. "Uh-oh. How so?"

"It was stupid. He was trying to be nice, and I got mad at him."

"About what?"

Brianne went ahead and told her the whole story, feeling embarrassed at first, but talking about it helped. She could only say what Austin had actually said, not all the things she thought he was thinking.

Her mom held her when she was finished, and after a few moments she assured her everything would be fine. "You know what the great thing is about girl-moments?"

"What?"

"Boys rarely understand them and think much about it. By tomorrow, if you go back to your normal self, Austin will too."

"But what about tonight? He's probably expecting me to come over. I don't know if I can face him again so soon."

"Go call him," she said. "If you're really over it, then there's no reason to avoid him."

She didn't respond.

"Are you over it?"

"I don't know."

"He's right, Brianne. You need to believe what he said."

"But it's not true! I'm not as pretty as Sarah!"

"Oh, honey," she said, taking her into her arms again as she began to cry. "Yes, you are."

"Not to boys!"

"Austin thinks so. He's a boy."

She felt like she was talking to a brick wall. First with Austin, and now with her mom. Why couldn't they just say what she knew to be true?

"Brianne, you can't compare yourself to others. If you do, there's always going to be someone who you think is prettier than you. If it's not your best friend, then it will be someone else. All you can be is who you are, the special and unique person God made you to be, and be happy with it. And not only with your looks, but with your personality and special talents and the unique qualities that make you who you are."

Her mom lifted her chin to force her to look at her. "You are pretty, Brianne. And you're caring and honest, and fun and sweet, and a great big sister, and an awesome friend—even to girls who aren't always nice to you; and boys who asked out your best friend instead of you. There's a lot more to beauty than what's on the surface, and you have it all, sweetheart. There are a lot of pretty girls who can't say that."

"I'm sorry I lied to the nurse today," she said.

"I understand. I think I did that a time or two myself, but don't try to avoid your friends or an issue when it comes up. That just delays the problem or makes it worse. You need to be honest with people—for yourself and for them."

Her mom went on to tell her about a time she hadn't been honest with her dad about something while they were dating and how it had blown up into this huge thing when it could have been dealt with much easier in the beginning.

"So I should either call Austin and talk about this more, or just let it go and move on?"

"Yes. You can use the phone in my bedroom if you want privacy."

"Okay," she said. Her mom kissed her on the forehead and left the room. Brianne thought about how she was feeling and realized Austin had already told her what he honestly thought, so there was no point in talking to him about it more. She just needed to believe what he said.

Going to her parents' bedroom, she closed the door and went to the phone on the night stand beside the bed. Brianne loved her mom and dad's room. The rest of the house was small and somewhat cluttered, simply because they had seven people living in a three bedroom house with only one central living room and a small kitchen and dining area. But her mom had gone to great lengths to make this her and Daddy's private space where she and her siblings were not allowed to play, jump on the bed, or use the phone unless given specific permission. The bedroom had all white furniture, and her mom had a blue and white comforter on the bed with lots of fluffy pillows and shams and a white canopy-like curtain that framed the headboard.

Sitting in a chair on the other side of the night stand and beside the doorway to the small bathroom, she asked God to help her through this and then she punched in Austin's number and waited for someone to pick up. His mom did after a few rings, and she asked if she could speak to Austin.

"Sure. Is that you, Brianne?"

"Yes."

"Hang on. I'll get him."

There was a long pause and then Austin's voice finally came on the line. She told him why she was calling, and he said he had been expecting her to come over tonight.

"I meant to ask you earlier, but I forgot."

"It's fine with me, but if you don't want to, that's okay," he replied.

"No. I want to. I really need to practice. I didn't have much of a chance this weekend."

"Okay. Can you get a ride, or do you need one?"

"I think my mom or dad can drive me. I'll call back if they can't. Is six-thirty still fine?"

"Yeah, I'll be here. We could work on that math too. Did you get that?"

"Yes."

"Could you help me? I was so lost."

"Sure."

"I was going to have you show me on the way home but then—. Are you okay?"

"Yeah, I'm fine. I'm sorry I didn't believe what you said. That was sweet, Austin."

"And true," he restated. "You know that, right?"

"Yeah, thanks."

He spoke again, sounding more nervous about what he wanted to say this time. "I was thinking about what I said to you and asking myself what made me let Sarah know how I felt about her, and yet not doing the same thing with you, and you know what it came down to for me?"

"What?"

"I think she's pretty and sweet, and all the same things you are, but she's not my pastor's daughter. Your dad is great, but that intimidates me a little bit, and I'm sure I'm not the only one."

"So no one's ever going to want to date me because my dad is a pastor?"

"No, I'm sure plenty will want to, but it will take a brave one to actually do it."

"And you're not that brave?"

"Well, you have this no-boyfriend policy now, remember?"

Brianne didn't know what to say. What was Austin saying?

"So anyway," he said, "that's a little insight from your best friend. See you later?"

"Yeah, I'll be there."

She hung up the phone and sat there for a minute, thinking about what Austin had confessed. Part of her didn't believe him—he'd only said that to be a good friend and make her feel better. But Austin was usually honest. If he didn't like her, he wouldn't want to be around her, and if he did consider her to be a friend, he wouldn't lie to her.

She went to the kitchen to ask her mom if she or Daddy could drive her over tonight, and her mom said one of them would. "Is everything all right now?"

"Yes. I apologized and said I believe him."

Her mom smiled. "I'm glad, honey. Austin is a good friend for you to have."

"I know," she said and laughed. "When I thought about who might become my new best friend this year, I never thought it would be Austin."

"Just because he's a boy, or for another reason?"

"Mostly that, but also because I never saw us as having a lot in common before, but I guess we do."

When she went to his house later, she wasn't sure she had ever been as anxious to see him. Being mad at him like she'd been this afternoon was unusual, and since she didn't have a reason to be mad in the first place, she realized how much she was enjoying her time with him this year. They had a different friendship than she and Sarah did, but she liked it for what it was.

After they had gone over their lines in the play and she had helped him with his math, he said his family had seen a really funny movie this weekend. "Do you want to stay and watch it with me, or at least part of it?"

She had planned to go home at eight, so she decided to call and ask if she could stay longer. Her dad said it was fine, and then Pastor Doug took the phone from her to tell her dad he could bring her home. They were still talking when she left the room and went back to tell Austin she could stay.

Austin's younger brother and sister watched most of it with them, and his mom and dad joined them about halfway through. It was really funny, and being with Austin and his family had a comfortable feel to it. She'd gotten to know them pretty well during the past two years, and their families had done things together in the past, but this was the first time she had spent time with all of them by herself.

When Pastor Doug drove her home, Austin went along too, and sitting between her youth pastor and his son in the cab of the older pickup truck had kind of a strange feeling to it. She didn't feel uncomfortable, but it wasn't something she had experienced before, and she wondered if it was the same kind of feeling Austin got when he thought about having his pastor's daughter as his girlfriend.

Arriving at the house, Austin got out of the truck and she followed him. He walked her up the front steps and said good night to her there. She thanked him for helping her with her lines and asking her to stay for the movie.

"Anytime, Brianne," he said. "That's what best friends are for, right?"

She smiled. "Absolutely."

Chapter Thirteen

On the night of the winter play, Brianne felt nervous, but she knew her part well. She always felt nervous before she did stuff like this, but not so much during the performance.

"I wish we could skip this part," she told Austin backstage when he came to find her and asked how she was doing.

"Yeah, me too," he said. "You're going to do great though. Last night you were perfect."

The first dress rehearsal on Saturday hadn't gone so well, but last night she hadn't messed up once. "Thanks for practicing with me more on Sunday," she said. "I know you must be sick of all my lines by now. Emma's such a brat."

He laughed. "No, I won't miss Emma, but I'll miss practicing with you."

She smiled and they exchanged a look that was becoming familiar to her. He had first looked at her that way last week when he said good night to her after she had stayed to watch the movie at his house. She didn't know for sure, but it seemed like Austin was looking at her in a special sort of way.

He wished her good luck and then walked to where he needed to get ready for his entrance onto the stage in a few minutes. She still had ten more minutes to wait.

"Hey, you," she heard a voice behind her say. She turned and saw Sarah standing there, and she squealed, but someone promptly shushed her because the performance had already started and they weren't that far from the stage.

"Sorry," she whispered and then turned back to Sarah and gave her a hug. "What are you doing here?"

"I wanted to come, but I wasn't sure if I could, so I didn't say anything. But here I am. My dad drove me right after dinner."

Brianne felt like she might cry, but she couldn't ruin her stage makeup. "Thank you," she said simply. "It means a lot to me, really."

"And you coming to my birthday party and meeting Ryan meant a lot to me, Brianne. I'm going to go find our seats, but I wanted to let you know I'm here."

"Is Ryan here too?"

"No. Just me and my dad. Are you going out somewhere afterwards? We can probably come too."

"Yes. I'm meeting my family and Austin's by the left stage door. I'll try not to take too long changing. Don't leave without at least saying good-bye, okay?"

"We'll stay," she said. "You look great. Have fun."

Brianne did have fun, and she only messed up one line, but it wasn't enough that anyone would know. Everyone else did well also, including Austin. Because her final part was after his, he was waiting for her when she came off the stage during her most dramatic and touching scene where her character loses her chance to win because someone says something about her that isn't true, and she learns a lesson about using her words about others more carefully.

"You were great," Austin said, giving her a hug.

She smiled. "That was so fun."

They hung around backstage together until it was time for them to do their curtain call at the end of the play. And because they were in the same group of actors and actresses who had unsuccessfully competed in the contest, they stood beside each other holding hands when they took their bows, which they hadn't done during the dress rehearsals.

Brianne had a strange feeling the whole time Austin was holding her hand, and she noticed him give it an extra squeeze just before he released it and they exited the stage. They had to go to separate areas to get out of their wardrobes, and she didn't see him again until she was headed for the area where their families and Sarah would be waiting for them. She had changed into her pink jeans and a white sweater but left her hair done up the fancy way Emma had worn it for the reading of her essay to Santa's grandson.

Austin was waiting for her inside the stage door, and he had flowers for her. Taking them from him, she didn't know what to say. She would have expected to get flowers from Sarah, but from Austin? That wasn't like him. He had never given her anything except for her birthday last year when she had invited him to her roller skating party, and it had only been a gift card.

"Thank you," she said, taking the pink roses from him and trying not to make a big deal out of it. "Did you know Sarah is here?"

"I saw her when I went out to get the flowers from my mom." He didn't seem as affected by Sarah's unexpected presence as he would have in the past. She supposed that was because of Ryan. If he did still have feelings for Sarah, they had to be put on hold for now.

"Were you surprised?" she asked. "I forgot to tell you she was here."

"I knew she might come. She told me in the last letter she wrote to me and said if she didn't make it, to tell you she really wanted to be here."

"Keeping secrets from me? Friends don't do that."

"They do if it's a good secret."

Not knowing what to say, she smiled and walked ahead of him to open the door. Brooke and Marissa were there, and they had flowers for her also. They couldn't stay but told her she'd done a really good job.

Stepping over to her family, she received hugs from her mom and dad and then Beth held out her arms, so she received a sweet hug from her also. "You look so beautiful, Bree," Beth said. "I clapped for you."

"Thank you, sweetie. I heard you clapping."

"Can I smell your flowers?"

"Sure," she said, holding the pink roses close to her nose.

"They're from Austin, aren't they?"

"Yes. Aren't they pretty?"

Beth nodded and they all began walking toward the outside doors. Sarah came over to link elbows with her.

"You were so great!" she said. "How could you play such a mean girl when you're nothing like that?"

She laughed. "I don't know. I guess I've seen enough girls who act like that for real."

"I have flowers for you too, but I left them in the car because I figured you would already have your hands full here."

"My mom got me some too, but she put them in a vase and set them in my room this afternoon. When she said I would be getting more here, I thought, 'From who?', but I guess she was right. I wasn't sure if Brooke and Marissa were coming, and I about fainted when I saw you!"

"I guess Austin is good at keeping secrets."

"Why did you tell him?"

"In his last letter he went on and on about how great you were going to be tonight, and he said I should come. Didn't he tell you he invited me?"

"No."

They had reached the van, and Sarah left her side to go with her dad to their car, saying she would see her in a few minutes. Brianne helped Beth get into the van and then sat beside her. Laying her flowers in her lap, she felt amazed by what Sarah had said. And she felt even more amazed Austin knew Sarah might be coming and yet had said nothing to her about it.

When they arrived at the restaurant, there was a long table reserved for them. Pastor Doug instructed her and Austin to sit in the middle across from each other, and everyone filled in around them. Sarah sat on her right side and Beth on her left. They ordered dessert, and she shared a brownie sundae with Sarah and Beth because they were so huge here. Austin got one just for himself, but he couldn't finish all of it.

Everyone was talking constantly, and Brianne was chatting equally with everyone within hearing-distance, but her eyes were on Austin much of the time. He seemed happy Sarah was here, but he wasn't looking at her as he often had in the past. It didn't matter to Brianne one way or the other, but she was curious about what Austin was thinking.

Saying good-bye to Sarah was hard because she didn't know when she would be seeing her again, but she thanked her for coming and for the flowers. They all left shortly after that, and Brianne still had tears in her eyes as they were walking out. She hadn't wanted to cry in front of everyone, but holding it in was too much.

Austin had fallen back to walk beside her, and he noticed the tears on her cheeks she had given up trying to brush away. He put his arm around her shoulder in a buddy-like way and leaned his head against hers.

"You'll see her again soon," he said. "Nothing keeps you two away from each other for long."

"I know. It's just hard. I miss her so much."

He didn't say anything. He just let her be sad.

"Thanks for inviting her to come," she said when they were almost to the van.

"She told you?"

"Yes. That was sweet. I thought about asking her myself, but I didn't want her to feel bad if she couldn't."

"Best friends shouldn't miss stuff like this."

"Do you really think I'm still her best friend, even now that she has Ryan?"

"Yes. She told me in one of her letters she feels closer to you now than she did when she was still living here."

"She's told me that too."

"Are you going to believe her?"

She smiled and spun away from him when he started to tickle her.

"See you tomorrow," she said, jogging over to the van.

"Good night. Practice your flute when you get home."

She laughed. They had a band concert tomorrow, and Miss Duncan had been frustrated with them today and told them all they needed to go home and practice. "I haven't even touched it, and I'm definitely not going to now."

She was really tired by the time they got home, but she did take out her Bible and devotional book after she had crawled into bed. She didn't start a new lesson but looked back at one she remembered doing, feeling drawn to it again. She knew she had found the right one when she saw the verse at the top that said, *Delight yourself in the LORD and he will give you the desires of your heart. Psalm 37:4*

One of the things she had been thinking about concerning Austin was, 'If he likes me as more than a friend and tries to take our friendship to something more than it is now, do I want that? Do I want to have a boyfriend right now or anytime soon if that becomes a possibility, or do I really want to wait until I'm sixteen?'

She knew she wanted to wait, but she wanted to get to know Austin better and have a deeper friendship with him. Not as boyfriend and girlfriend, at least not yet, but as more than casual friends too. Was there such a place In between? She wanted that in-between stage with Austin right now. That was the desire of her heart, so maybe God would give it to her. The writer's insight confirmed that to some extent, but she also pointed out something Brianne knew she needed to remember:

This is a really cool verse full of a wonderful promise: God will give you the desires of your heart. But what does it mean to 'Delight yourself in the LORD'--the condition of this promise? In simple terms, to delight in something is to enjoy it. Like if you really enjoy ballet dancing, you delight in learning, doing, and watching it. Or if you like reading, you delight in the stories you read. To delight in someone is similar. You delight in your best friend because you enjoy the time you spend together, or you delight in your family because they bring a certain joy to your heart that is hard to find elsewhere.

When we delight in God, it means we enjoy Him. We enjoy the relationship we have with Him. We find Him to be delightful. Is that how you would describe God?

Brianne thought about that, and she wasn't sure. She had come to a better understanding of God during the last few months, but a lot of it was still in her head. She had been asking God for help, and she had seen Him take care of her and provide in many ways, but she didn't know if she could say she was delighting in Him and finding Him delightful.

She highlighted some sentences near the end she knew she needed to apply to her relationship with God and to her growing friendship with Austin.

It's about having a vital, growing, and exciting relationship with Him. One where you believe Him and trust Him with all of your heart with whatever you're facing...

I'm not sure what I'm facing, Jesus. What's going on with Austin? Why did he invite Sarah for me and give me flowers? Why did I feel strange when he was holding my hand? Why did I feel better about Sarah leaving after talking to him? Are we friends like me and Sarah are, or is it different somehow?

I want to have the right desires, and I want to have a greater desire for you. I think I'm on the right path, but I think I have a long way to go too. Help! I don't know what's going on or what I should do about it.

Chapter Fourteen

After Brianne had prayed about her friendship with Austin and asked Jesus to take her into a more complete and delightful relationship with Him, she turned out the light. The play had been really fun, and she was glad she had decided to take on the more challenging role. But more than the performance tonight, she had enjoyed the time she spent practicing with Austin. He was always so encouraging, especially on Sunday when she had been freaking out and saying she couldn't do it. He'd taken the time to practice with her instead of playing a new video game with J.T.

For some reason he believed in her, and it showed. And the more she thought about it, the more she realized he had always been that way. When she had first moved here, her family had gone over to his house a lot so their families could get to know each other, and he had never acted like she was intruding on his space as the youth pastor's son. He'd made her a part of it. He had accepted her for who she was right from the beginning.

And then this year with Sarah being gone, he had been there, filling the gap so easily she thought could never be filled. He wasn't like Sarah. He wasn't even a girl, but he had been a friend in the way she needed him to be. He had helped her through the ordeal with Ashlee and Silas. He hadn't let her think less of herself than she should. He'd been there to help her with the lines for the play when she had simply asked him.

And tonight when she had seen him before, during, and after the play, he had been exactly what she needed; giving her flowers and telling her she'd done great; inviting Sarah to come and keeping it a secret; comforting her in the right way after Sarah was gone. In a way she felt like it had all been a dream. She hadn't expected any of it, and yet he had been exactly what she needed to make the night absolutely perfect.

She felt tired in the morning. Silas and Danielle were at the end of her driveway as she rushed out to meet them. They hadn't been able to attend the play because the church their parents were starting had a Christmas festival at the elementary school where they had been meeting. They asked her how it had gone, and she told them the truth.

"I wish we could have been there," Silas said.

"That's okay. I had a good fan club. Sarah was there."

"Austin said she might be. He was really hoping she would make it."

"She did, and I was surprised. It was fun."

The bus pulled up and opened the door for them. They took their usual seats, and Brianne found herself feeling excited about seeing Austin. But it wasn't in an 'I want to be his girlfriend' kind of way like she had felt about various guys she knew. It was more like how she had always looked forward to seeing Sarah and having time with her. She had seen him last night, and she hadn't missed him like she missed Sarah right now, but she knew if she wasn't going to be seeing him for awhile, she would.

He appeared tired also as he got on the bus and sat beside her, but he told her 'good morning' and then promptly turned around and asked Silas and Danielle if she had told them how awesome she'd done last night.

When he turned back around, she playfully slugged him in the arm. "Would you stop? You're embarrassing me!"

"I will not. My dad was talking last night about us doing a play at church next Christmas and giving you the lead role."

"What?"

"You heard me. My dad won't let that kind of talent go to waste."

She rolled her eyes and thought, 'What am I getting myself into?' But at the same time she felt secretly thrilled. They had done a few skits and things before in the children's programs, and she'd had bit-parts, but doing a youth play for church could be a lot of fun—if they could get enough people to participate. The attendance at youth group had been better lately, but they were still hoping for their group to grow to about twice the size it was now. She'd heard her dad and Pastor Doug talking about it, and they had been trying new things, but they were both frustrated with the lack of attendance, especially in the upper grades.

She had a good day and had to go back to the school that night for their band concert. Brianne knew she played her part well, but she heard a lot of wrong notes being played around her. She walked out with Brooke, Marissa, and Austin after the other bands and choirs had performed, and they were laughing about one of the songs they did really horrible on. She whispered in case any of the trumpet players were within hearing-distance, but some of the parts of the Christmas medley had been so bad, she doubted the audience recognized the familiar songs.

They waited for their families to come out along with the rest of the crowd, and Brooke and Marissa's did before hers or Austin's. Once it was just the two of them, Austin had an interesting request.

"Do you want to do something with me on Saturday?"

"Like what?"

"I don't know, whatever."

"Like go somewhere, you mean?"

"Sure. The movies, roller skating, bowling, whatever you want."

She stared at him for a moment. He had never asked her that before. "You mean, like a date?"

"No. I know you don't date. As a friend. Like you and Sarah used to do all the time."

"Okay. Sure. I'll have to ask, but it will probably be okay. I have to babysit in the evening because of the Christmas dinner at church, but maybe right after lunch?"

"That's fine. We could go earlier and get lunch somewhere too. You pick what you want to do, and we'll figure it out from there."

She saw her mom and dad coming, so she gave him her answer quickly. "Let's go to a movie. I haven't seen that new Christmas one everyone says is good. Have you?"

"No."

"Okay. See you tomorrow."

She didn't say anything to her mom and dad about it until after they got home and Beth and her brothers were in bed. She had brushed her teeth and gotten into her pajamas, but she went out to the living room to talk to them, feeling a bit awkward since this was the first time Austin had ever asked her to spend time with him outside of school, church, or at his house.

"Is his whole family going?" her dad asked.

"No. Just me and him."

"So it's a date?"

She smiled. "No. He knows I don't date. It's just a friend thing—like me and Sarah used to do."

"If you want to go, it's fine. We have that Christmas dinner in the evening. Did you remember that?"

"Yes. He said we could go earlier."

"Okay. Let us know what you decide on."

Brianne wasn't sure why, but she decided not to tell anyone else about it. Not even Silas or Brooke when she saw them several times the following day and on Friday: their last day of school before Winter Break.

When she got home on Friday afternoon she finished wrapping the Christmas presents she had gotten for Sarah and Joel, and her mom took her to the Post Office to mail them. She had meant to do it sooner, but this had been a busy week. She had gone with Sarah's idea about getting a picture frame, but not for Joel. She got one for Sarah instead and put a picture of them in it Ryan had taken with her camera on Sarah's birthday. It was a really great picture, and she'd had the same picture framed for herself.

For Joel she had decided against the picture idea. Instead she had gotten him a devotional book for junior high guys and also a one-time-use camera with a note on it that said:

> I don't have any recent pictures of you. Have your family take some and then send this back to me.

On Saturday there was a one o'clock showing of the movie she wanted to see, so they decided to go to lunch first and then see the movie. Austin's dad drove them to Dairy Queen that was just across the street from the movie theater, and he would be coming to pick them up at three.

While they ate their cheeseburgers and fries, Austin asked if she was looking forward to going to visit her grandparents, and she said she was. She always enjoyed being there. They were leaving tomorrow right after church.

"Are you staying with your dad's family or your mom's?"

"My mom's. My other grandparents live in Seattle and we'll go down to see them on Christmas Day and probably one or two other days, but they have a really small house and one of my aunts lives with them with her kids, so there isn't room for us to stay there overnight."

"Which grandparents do you like better?"

"I like them both, but we've spent more time with my mom's. They're the ones I stayed with for a week last summer."

"Do you think you'll do that again?"

"Yeah, maybe. I told you I might go see Sarah and she might come here, didn't I?"

"Yes."

"That would be really fun, or maybe she could go with me to my grandparents'," she said. "I liked being there, but it was a little boring sometimes without anyone my age. And you're going to camp, right?"

"Planning on it."

When they were done eating, they walked through the cold December air to the movie theater. Once they were in their seats in the half-filled room, she let Austin hold the popcorn. She really wasn't hungry for much. Being there with him reminded her of times she had been here with Sarah, but it felt different too. She had been thinking about her prayers from earlier in the week, and she wasn't sure what was going on between her and Austin, but she felt comfortable being here with him.

The movie was good like everyone said, and seeing it with Austin was fun. Some of it was funny, some of it serious, and it had a few tear-jerking moments near the end before the big happy ending. One of the touching parts for Brianne was when the two girls had to say good-bye to each other who had become good friends while their families had been spending Winter Break at a ski resort. They knew they might never see each other again because they lived on opposite sides of the country.

Austin leaned over and spoke the exact words in her ear she was thinking: "At least Sarah isn't that far away."

She turned and smiled at him, adding another thing she was thinking. "And Sarah isn't my only friend."

Chapter Fifteen

On Sunday morning, Brianne finished packing her bags before they left for church. Her mom and dad wanted to leave as soon as possible after they got home today, and she knew her mom would need her help with getting the rest of her brothers' and Beth's things together. She felt excited about going, seeing her grandparents and cousins, and especially about Christmas coming up in three more days, but she knew she would miss home too, especially seeing her friends every day.

She had several gifts to give out that morning. She had already given Brooke, Silas, and Marissa their gifts on Friday because they weren't always at church on Sunday mornings. Marissa had been coming to youth group as long as she didn't have an away basketball game on Thursday, but her family did a lot together on the weekends, so she was often out of town or just busy on Sundays. They were going to southern California to visit family for Christmas, and they'd left yesterday.

Brooke had been coming to youth group also, but her family still attended the church in Longview. Brooke only came to Rivergate on Sunday mornings if she spent the night at her house. And Silas had been going with his family to the new church off and on now that they had a fair amount of teens coming. Danielle had been coming to their church every Sunday, however. She needed to be a part of a strong youth group right now, and she really loved Pastor Doug and Mrs. Lockhart and appreciated all they were doing to help her. Brianne had a gift for her, and she gave it to her while they were waiting for the worship time to begin.

"Do you want me to open it now?" she asked.

"Yes. I have something to say about it."

Danielle opened the small box and took out the silver LOVE ring. Brianne held out her hand and said, "It's just like the one my friend gave me at Thanksgiving. He gave it to me to help me remember God loves me, and I wanted to give you one for the same reason."

Danielle smiled and gave her a hug. "Thank you, Brianne. I'll wear it all the time."

Brianne had gotten Emily a book she picked up at the Christian bookstore, and Emily thanked her when she gave it to her after class. And she gave Ashlee a CD of a Christian band she knew she liked. Ashlee seemed surprised she had gotten her something, and she didn't have anything to give her in return, but she thanked her and told her to have a nice break and time with her grandparents.

Brianne waited until after church to give Austin his gift. Their families were usually the last to leave, and she caught him when no one else was around. He had gone back to the youth room to play drums like he often did, although as she entered the room, he was on his way out to find her.

"Oh good, you're still here," he said.

"Of course I am. You didn't think I'd leave without saying good-bye, did you?"

"No, I guess not. Especially since you haven't given me my gift yet."

She laughed. "Oh? Expecting one, are you?"

"Hey, you can't give something to Ashlee and not to me."

She held out the gift she had been hiding behind her back. She had covered a shoe box with wrapping paper, so all he had to do was lift the lid.

"You got me shoes?" he teased before taking it from her.

"No. Open it."

She'd had a hard time deciding what to get him and had ended up getting several things: a music gift card, the same guys' devotional book she had sent to Joel, and a t-shirt with a skateboard on the back and the phrase:

I love God, God loves me, and we love to skate.

He laughed when he read it. "Thanks. But now I feel bad I didn't get you anything."

"You don't have to get me anything."

"Oh, wait. I think I did get you something. What did I do with that?"

She laughed. "You got me something?"

"Yes," he said, sounding like a seventh-grade boy.

"Don't take that tone with me, Austin Douglas Lockhart."

"Don't call me that, or I might not give it to you." He took something out of his back pocket and held it up for her to see. It looked like a folded piece of paper.

"What did you do, write me something?"

"Don't take that tone with me, Brianne Rebekah Carmichael. Do you want it or not?"

"What is it?"

He unfolded the blue paper and pretended like he was just now seeing what it contained for himself. "Mmmm, I wonder what this is?"

She tried to grab it away from him, but he smiled and held it out of her reach. "Oh, it looks like a concert schedule."

He turned the paper, and she saw the names of two of her favorite Christian groups written in bold letters at the top. "Are they coming to someplace around here?"

"I don't know. Let's see. Oh, yes. They are in Portland...on...February 14th."

"They're coming on my birthday?"

He looked at her and smiled. "I guess so."

She wasn't sure what to say. Was he planning to go? Had he gotten them tickets? "And this has something to do with my Christmas present because...?"

He refolded the paper and smiled. "Because we're going, if you want."

"Me and you? You got tickets?"

"No, they don't go on sale until next month, but yes, I'd like to take you, and I thought maybe we could meet Sarah and Ryan there. If you want to invite Silas and Brooke and whoever else, that's fine, but they have to pay their own way. I'm only paying for me and you."

Putting her hands on her hips, she challenged his motives. "Is this a tricky way of getting me to go on a date with you?"

"No. I don't date. I'm only thirteen," he said as if her question was completely ridiculous. "And I especially don't date my pastor's daughter."

She smiled and knew there was no way she could tell him she didn't want to go. She loved the music, she would be seeing Sarah again, and she would enjoy going to a concert with Austin and maybe some of her other friends too. Their youth group couldn't usually go to concerts during the school year because in smaller cities like Portland, the concerts were often in the middle of the week and they would get home too late on a school night.

"I'll have to ask," she said. "But if my dad says it's okay, I'd love to go."

"My dad already talked to him."

"He did?"

"Yep. My dad said we should ask your mom and dad before I asked you."

Brianne was amazed her parents knew about this but hadn't said anything. "You talked to my dad? I thought you weren't that brave?"

"I'm not. My dad talked to him."

She laughed and gave him a hug. "Thank you. I can't believe you even thought to do this."

She released him, and they began walking toward the door at the end of the hall. He said something she hadn't thought about yet.

"I wonder if we'll have all of our classes together next semester."

"I don't know," she said. "I hope so."

"Do you?"

"Yes. I can't believe I'm saying this, but this year has been really fun—most of the time anyway."

"You thought you would be sick of me by now?"

"No, I didn't mean that. I meant I thought I'd never survive without Sarah, but God knew things I didn't."

"What things?"

"Lots of things, but mostly He knew what a good friend you would be to me."

"You have lots of friends, Brianne. Not just me."

"I know, but you're kind of my favorite."

He looked embarrassed. "Why? Because I got you concert tickets?"

"No. Because you're fun, but not an idiot, and you're serious, but not too serious. And after spending a gazillion hours with you since September, I'm not sick of you, you're my best friend!"

He opened the door, and she stepped outside. They walked to the van where her mom was getting Beth settled and her brothers were being their usual rowdy selves, but her dad hadn't come outside yet.

"Hi, Austin," her mom said when she saw they had come up behind her. "Did you like your gifts?"

"Yes. She was almost as thoughtful as me."

Her mom smiled. "Yours is hard to beat."

"I can't believe you and Daddy knew," Brianne said. "Why didn't you tell me?"

"And spoil the surprise? That wouldn't be any fun."

Brianne saw her dad coming toward the van, and she turned back to tell Austin good-bye. "I guess I'll see you in a couple of weeks."

"I'll be here when you get back."

"Okay. Bye," she said, giving him another hug.

"Merry Christmas, Brianne."

"Merry Christmas," she replied.

She got into the van beside Beth, and he closed the door before stepping away. Her dad waved to Austin and got into the van himself.

"Are we all here?" he asked.

"Yes," they all answered.

On the way home, Brianne recalled what she said to Austin about him being her favorite friend, and she knew it was true. All week she had been sort of nervous about seeing Austin and wondering how she should act around him, but whenever she was actually with him, it had been easy and fun.

She still didn't know if he saw her strictly as a friend or if he did have some hopeful feelings about her, but she had decided it didn't matter. God was helping her to be herself and enjoy their friendship for what it was, and she supposed He would help her with that no matter how Austin acted or what he said to her.

Her dad didn't say anything to her about the concert until later. She had finished helping her mom make a simple lunch for all of them to have before they loaded up the van and hit the road. Going back to her room to change out of her dressy clothes before she ate, she met her dad in the hallway, and he took advantage of the private moment.

"Did Austin tell you about the gift he has for you?"

"Yes," she said. "Thanks for saying it was okay."

He gave her a hug. "I hope you have fun."

"But you're glad it's still a couple of months away?"

"Yes and no."

His answer surprised her. Ever since she had turned twelve he'd been telling her to not grow up too fast. "Did I just hear you say 'no'?"

"Yes and no," he said again. "Yes because I'm not too anxious for you to be thirteen, but no because I know you'll be fine. You're growing up whether I like it or not."

"I'm trying not to grow up too fast."

"I know, and I'm proud of you for all the good choices you're making."

Her dad went to load up the car, and she went to change. While she did so and finished getting her things together for the trip, she realized making good choices wasn't just something to do to make her mom and dad proud of her, but it was something she wanted to do for herself. Growing up was complicated, but if she kept following God and His ways, going to Him when she felt hurt or confused, and loving others the best she knew how, then she would always have what she needed to make it through anything.

She realized Jesus was whispering something to her heart over and over, every day in every situation:

Anything you need, Brianne, I'm here.

I love to hear from my readers

Write me at:

living_loved@yahoo.com

Titles in the Heaven in my Heart series:

Closer Than Ever
Anything You Need
A Real Friend
Don't Let Go
Face To Face
Keeping It Real
By Your Side
Let It Shine

66547577R00084

Made in the USA
San Bernardino, CA
12 January 2018